Best Blessing of
Shirley Sealy

'4

For every tear there
is a smile.
For every joy, a sorrow,
And for every hurt there
is a healing.
Shirley Sealy

Laughter and Tears
... the best years

Laughter and Tears
...the best years

shirley sealy

© 1983 by Randall Book Company
ISBN: 0-934126-28-3
All rights reserved.

First Printing January 1983
Printed in the United States of America
Publishers Press, Salt Lake City, Utah

Randall Book Company
Orem, Utah

To my husband, L. Milton Sealy,
my children and grandchildren
who helped me find the way.

1

"**M**other, my wedding dress! It's like a picture out of my dreams!"

"And you look like a dream, Molaine. What a beautiful bride you'll be."

"I can't believe I'm really getting married."

"My oldest daughter." There was a lump in Muriel Norman's throat, and she blinked back the tears as she watched Molaine turn around in front of the mirror. "Just a few days now and you'll no longer be Molaine Norman, you'll be Mrs. Randolph McGregary. My first married daughter."

Molaine's eyes brightened as she looked at herself in the mirror and repeated the title. "Mrs. Randolph McGregary. Can you believe it?" She laughed out loud, watching her own reaction in the mirror. "Imagine, Mrs. Randolph McGregary. Doesn't even sound like me. Mrs. Randy McGregary or Mrs. Mac . . . I think I like Mrs. Mac the best. Do you think I can expect people to call me Mrs. Mac?"

"People will call you what they want to; what you answer to is up to you. What difference does it make as long as you have Randy?"

"That's right." She turned and looked at her mother. "Oh, Mother, I'm really so frightened. I wish Randy would wait two more years while I graduate. I would like my degree and my teaching certificate."

"Oh, please Molaine, not now. The wedding invitations are all out, the hall is rented, your line is almost finished . . . not now, dear. The wedding must go on, haven't you heard?"

Molaine turned suddenly to face her mother. There was stress in her face, emotion in her voice. "Why must the wedding go on?"

"Well, I don't know. It's just a saying, you know, like the show must go on. I didn't mean anything by the remark."

"But I want to know why. Can't you tell me why? What if I decided not to get married right now? What if I . . ."

"Molie, please dear. Don't frighten me. We've worked so hard . . ."

"Is work more important than my happiness?"

"We've worked for your happiness. We've solved most of the problems now . . ."

"There have been so many . . . hurt feelings, how many bridesmaids, where to hold it, the colors. It seems like I haven't seen Randy since our engagement. We've done nothing but solve problems and worry about other people's feelings. I thought this was my wedding."

"It is dear. But this is my first wedding. We've had a few problems, but I think you've been wise."

"I don't know if I'm wise or not. I don't know if I want to get married or not." Molaine reached for the zipper of her dress, and her mother automatically stepped close to help her. Her mother didn't say anything, but there was a look on her face that cut into Molaine deeper than anything she could have said. "I'm sorry, Mother, but I just don't know anymore. Maybe I don't want to get married anymore." Stepping out of the dress, she dropped it into her mother's arms, escaped through the door, into the hall, up the steps at the far end and to her own room.

"How can you do this to your mother?" she asked herself as she pulled a suitcase out of her closet and began to pack. "Only a few days ago I unpacked this suitcase, so excited to be home from college. Now all I want to do is run . . . run and hide and never think about the family or money or Randy or a w-wedding . . .

ever . . ." Grabbing a handful of socks and underwear, she shoved them into the suitcase and was on her way to get some things out of her closet when the telephone rang. She put her hands over her ears and went on. Then she heard her mother's voice.

"Mo . . . Molie, the telephone is for you."

That will be Randy, she thought. "I can't talk to Randy now!" Slamming her bag shut, she ran down the steps and out into the yard where she climbed into the old family car and drove away, a faint far-away sound of her mother's voice calling her name.

Shaking with emotion, tears blurring her vision, without knowing just where to go, she automatically turned the corner leading to the University. The car seemed to go of its own will born of habit. As she drove, the tears rolled down her face, and her body began to shake. "I'm so dumb," she said out loud to herself. "Randy is the best there is. If I run away now, there may never be another Randy in my life. He won't wait, he told me that. He's a mature man, ready to get married, and he wants a wife that is emotionally sound. That's what he said. But I'm not emotionally sound. I used to be, but I'm not now." She pressed her foot down harder on the gas and took two turns, skidding around the second, and found herself on the road to her old apartment. "Lucy, good old Lucy. Please be there; I need to talk, I need to talk so bad . . . ."

Molaine took hold of the doorknob and then remembered she didn't live there anymore and rang the doorbell. She heard a faint sound of singing inside as she recognized the familiar voice of Lucy as she came to open the door.

"Mo!!" Lucy threw her arms around her ex-roommate and hugged her. "Mo, how I've missed you. I can't believe how much I missed you." Releasing her, she took her by the arm. "Come on in and tell me all about your wedding plans. Everything is about ready, no?"

"No . . . I mean, well, the wedding . . . It's a perfect summer month, the time is right, the groom is . . . ."

"The groom is super, and you know it. I kinda' wish my waiting was over. You having a wedding and out of school for summer . . . and me just starting my dance class. I think I'll be going to school forever. Believe me, you've got it made."

"But we'll be back to school in the fall. Two more years for Randy, and he wants me to graduate . . ."

"I know, but you have summers off. Me, I go to school in the winter, spring, and fall and teach in the summer. Excuse me, Mo, but it's called feeling-sorry-for-myself time of year. But tell me about you. You know, I was just telling my dance class about you. I've got these lovesick girls in that class, and I just told them if they wanted to get the right guy, they had to shape up. Then I told them about you and Randy . . . the perfect couple. How's Randy holding up? He's pretty solid, but even the big ones go down just before the wedding."

"They do?"

"Sure, butterflies, the whole thing."

"Not Randy, he's the rock kind, stable to the end. I'm the one that's hard to live with."

"You're telling me. I lived with you, didn't I?"

"Oh, Lucy, was I so bad?" The tears were close to the surface again, but Lucy didn't seem to notice. She just pulled Molaine into her room and pushed her down on the bed.

"Of course not, you goofey girl. You're my favorite person in the whole world, next to Jeffrey, who won't be home from his mission for six more months. Now sit there while I separate these costumes and tell me all about the wedding. I want every detail."

"I forgot, Lucy, you're getting ready for your dance concert, aren't you?"

"We've got dress rehearsal tonight. I've been going mad. But I've got a few minutes, just talk, tell me everything."

"Well, I . . ." but Molaine didn't get anymore said because the telephone interrupted them. Lucy waved her apology and went to answer it.

From Lucy's half of the conversation, Molaine could tell the call was about dance details, and she knew this wasn't the time to talk to Lucy about a marriage that wasn't going to be. Getting up, she went to Lucy, kissed her on the cheek, waved her hand, and went toward the door.

"Hang on a minute," Lucy said into the phone and then put

her hand over the receiver. "Wait a minute, Mo. We didn't get to talk at all."

"I'll call you sometime, all right?"

"All right. You sure?"

"Sure."

Back in the car, Molaine drove to upper campus, parked the car in the parking lot, and walked across the grass to sit beside the spraying fountain in the center. She had to think.

How many times have Randy and I been right here, sitting right here where I am? She looked at her image in the moving water. *It was here he kissed me the night he proposed. I'll never forget his nervousness. I laughed and said: "Randy, we've talked about getting married all our lives. Can't you make it official without getting uptight?"*

"But, Molie, this is the real thing. We aren't kids anymore. It's time to get serious."

"It is, huh?" I went on laughing.

"Mo, please. This is serious."

"I know. But you look so funny when you are serious. What are you trying to say, Randy? As if I didn't know . . ."

And then he had proposed, stumbling into the words but finally coming out with asking her to marry him. But it hadn't been his words that had caused her to stop laughing and be serious. It was the look in his eyes. She could always tell what Randy was thinking by his eyes.

"Your eyes mirror your insides," she'd once told him.

"Then look and see how much you're loved."

Shutting her eyes, she got up and turned around, putting her back against the spray. *I don't want to see Randy's eyes when I tell him. I'll write him a letter. No, I'll call him . . . no, I'll just go away.* Getting up, she started walking. The lights came on, flooding the campus with a new brightness, taking away the dusk of late afternoon.

I've got to stop thinking about Randy. It's all over. I've known it for a long time, ever since we started planning the wedding. We haven't even seen each other. He's been working, and I've been working and planning and sewing and trying to keep peace among the aunts and his family and mine. Everybody wants their ideas in my wedding.

She started walking faster now even though she wasn't sure

of where she was going. The campus wasn't crowded, she could tell it was summer. It was summer, and she was supposed to be having a summer wedding, the way she had always planned. She kept on walking and found herself at the bottom of the steps that lead down. It was the way she had always walked home from her classes her freshman year. Randy was on his mission then.

Halfway down the steps she stopped to look below. It was getting darker now, and the trees were only dark forms. It was dangerous to linger on the steps after dark. There had been a lot of rapes on the steps—girls being pulled into the bushes. She ignored the warning and sat down on the edge of the sidewalk, letting her feet dangle down the hill.

The ideal couple, that's what Lucy said. She couldn't keep the thoughts out of her mind. *I wonder what she'll say when she knows I've run out? It's always been Randy. We've been together for so long. I waited while he went on his mission. Well, not exactly waited. I dated; there was Chris and Hank and . . . Hank was more romantic than Randy, but . . . but I can't go through with it. I can't. I don't feel anything anymore.*

It was full darkness, and the trees behind the sidewalk made errie shapes on the walk. The warning came again, something inside telling her it was dangerous to be here alone. But she wasn't ready to move. She hadn't decided where to go.

I can go to Grandma's house. She'll understand. I can stay with Grandma and Grandpa, and they won't ask questions or accuse me. I could go to California and try for that part in little theatre my instructor wanted me to go for. I could get a job . . . .

There was a movement in the trees behind her. Only reflections of the street light dented the darkness, but it wasn't enough. Someone or something moved again. Molaine froze. Suddenly she was frightened. She got up to make a run for the steps. She could sense that it was a figure of a man; it had to be a man . . . her stomach tied in a knot. She started to run . . . two arms grabbed her, and she let out a scream—screaming the name first on her mind.

"RANDY . . . RANDY!!!"

"Molaine?" The arms were strangely familiar. "Molaine, is it you?"

"Randy?" Some of the fear began to leave her. "Randy?"

"Yes. It's me. What are you doing here . . . here alone?" His arms tightened around her. She began to cry.

"Oh, Randy, I was so scared. I really was scared."

"You should be. What are you doing here alone?"

"I . . . I don't know. I had to leave . . . I . . . ran away."

"You ran away?"

"Yes, didn't Mother tell you when I didn't come to the phone?"

"I didn't phone."

"You didn't?"

"No. I had April call your house . . . little sisters, can't they do anything right? Didn't you get the message?"

"No. What was the message, Randy?"

"I just left word that I wouldn't be over, that I'd call you later."

"Then you didn't come to find me?"

"I didn't know you were gone. You didn't answer me. What are you doing here?"

"Well, I . . ." she moved out of his arms, but she was glad he held on to her hand. "Well, Randy . . . Mac, old boy . . . Randy . . . I was running out."

"You were what? You mean on our marriage?"

"Yes. You have to know. I have to tell you. Yes, I'm running out. You can hate me if you want to but . . ."

"But why?" It was strange, but even in the dim outline she could see that his eyes weren't like she imagined they would be . . . hurt and . . .

"Well, Randy . . . I just don't feel anything anymore. I'm sorry, but I don't. I guess I'm too young to get married. I'm too immature. I've decided I'll graduate first, teach high school for a while. I'm sorry, Randy. I hope you'll forgive me. It isn't you, it's just me."

"If you'll forgive me."

"What have I to forgive you for? You're the solid piece-of-the-rock kind. You have your head on straight, and you deserve someone better. You'll see, you'll be glad."

"Maybe I will."

"What?" This wasn't turning out at all like Molaine supposed it would.

"I said maybe I would be glad. This way I won't have to hurt you."

"You were going to hurt me?" She was puzzled. Randy started to laugh, and his laugh irritated her. "Is something funny?"

"It seems that way. You see, I was running out . . . on you."

"You were what?"

"You heard me. I ran out. I left. I wasn't going through with the marriage."

"Well, I'm glad I wasn't wrong about my feelings. I guess what I was feeling was that you didn't care for me anymore. Well, see you around . . ." Angry, she pulled her hand out of his and started down the steps. He took a big step and grabbed her hand again, pulling her toward the top of the path.

"It seems we were both feeling the same thing. Let's talk."

"I don't want to talk to you. I just want out."

"Come on, let's be mature, like everybody says. Little do they know, if we were mature, we wouldn't be getting married at all."

"Right. Now let's skip the emotion and sit down and talk like adults."

"I don't feel like an adult. I don't want to be an adult. That's part of the problem. I just want to be me, to have fun and laugh again. Getting married is too serious."

"That's what I thought. Come on, sit down."

"It's dangerous here on this walk."

"I know. We'll sit here in the light and talk, all right?"

"Why? I think we've said it all."

"Six years in grade school, three in junior high, three in high school, and two in college and then add two years of letters . . . I think we owe each other a good talk. Wouldn't you think?"

"We do go back a ways." He pulled her down beside him on a rock under the light of the upper campus, and she began to feel more comfortable. "All right, you tell me first. Don't worry about my feelings, just get it out."

"Yes, doctor. I'll just sit here and say whatever comes to my mind, all right?" She smiled, feeling the tension leave. "It's crazy the way you always have a calming effect on me."

"You do the same thing for me. Funny, I was so uptight I thought I just couldn't go through with it. It's a big responsibility . . . getting married. I started doubting my feelings, and then the responsibility got bigger. I thought I'd go away and see how I felt."

"Were you coming back?"

"I don't know." He looked off into the trees. "I couldn't figure out what happened. I thought I wanted to get married, and then I just wasn't sure. You have to be sure about a thing as big as marriage. You want me to be honest, don't you?"

"Yes. We have to be honest. If we can't say what we feel, then we haven't anything."

"Tell me, why were you running out?" He looked right at her.

"The same. Everybody planning my wedding, everybody wanting to make decisions for me. When I asked you about the plans, you didn't seem to care."

"What do I know about dresses and showers and invitations? I don't care about those things, Molaine."

"Not even for your own wedding?"

"Not really. I've tried to care about them, for you, but I don't really care. I just want you. I want to get married. I mean, I did want to get married. Then I got confused."

"You, confused?" Molaine started to laugh.

"Something funny?" He looked at her with the street light on her hair. He'd forgotten how pretty she was, how her face glowed when her laughter filled the air, how good he felt when he was with her.

"I think you're funny. Mr. piece-of-the-rock, Mr. Solid-Citizen Randy McGregary . . . you, confused?"

"I've been through my share of confusion, didn't you know?"

"What's this, a new side to Randy McGregary, the A-student valedictorian of his class. You always know where you're going and how to get there. How can you be confused?"

"I don't know." He shrugged. "It's love, I guess. I'm not ready for it."

"That makes two of us. What shall we do about it?"

"I think we should call it off."

"What will your folks say?"

"What will yours say?"

"Oh, Randy, they've already said it. Well, at least Mother said it, and I'm sure by now Dad has said it, too."

"Said what?" Then together they both said: *"You can't do this!"*

As they finished the sentence, they both laughed. They laughed loud, rocking back and forth, as if they'd been starving for a good laugh. They rocked back and forth with laughter.

"It's going to be a shock to the world, isn't it?"

"Sure is. Randy, everybody has been expecting us to get married since we were Mary and Joseph in the Christmas program in junior high school."

"That's right. I'd almost forgotten that. What made you remember the Mary and Joseph scene?"

"I don't know. I haven't thought about it for a long time. I was mad at you. I was so mad."

"I'll say you were. I've still got the bump where you hit me with my own cane."

"Oh, you have not. That's an exaggeration. Randy, you always exaggerate."

"No fun if you don't. But I've got the bump all right, want to feel it?" He leaned forward, the top of his head right under the street light. He parted his hair with his fingers and rubbed until he found the small swelling. "Hasn't ever gone away. I used to rub it at night when I was thinking of you, when I was on my mission."

She laughed again as she tried to find the spot on top of his head he was guiding her fingers to.

"It's right there, feel it now?" She moved her fingers slightly.

"Yeah, it is there. Randy, how silly."

"It's not silly, it's my bump, and it was a comfort to me. Kinda' like taking a hot water bottle to bed. Some of the Elders took a letter to bed, but me . . . I always had my bump. What was it you got mad at me for anyway?"

"You laughed at me. You said I wasn't beautiful. Scott had told me I was beautiful, and you made fun of him. You said I just looked stupid in that blue robe over my head."

"Well, you did. It was a heavy robe, and it smashed your hair. I always liked your hair."

"You did?"

"Sure. You know that." He looked at her quietly, the light picking up the glow in his eyes. He had that look, the one that always made her heart do funny things.

"Yes, I guess I know," she said softly. "But I like to hear you say it."

"You do?" They sat there looking at each other, and suddenly she was in his arms, and he was kissing her.

Randy's heart beat fast, and the old zing of what he'd always felt for her was back. He could feel her respond, and when they stopped kissing, he still held her tight. "Molie . . . Molie . . . what are we doing? We can't get out of this marriage. It wouldn't be legal."

"Legal? It wouldn't even be moral. I've never let anyone kiss me like that before. I've never kissed anyone like . . ."

"And you'd better not, ever. You crazy girl, you can't run out on me. You're stuck with me for life."

"But you were running."

"Only because I'd forgotten what you look and feel like. I was up to my neck in trying to make money stretch, and I didn't see you alone. And then when I did, we were deep in decorations and wedding dress and aunts and uncles. Molie, I didn't know you had so many aunts and all of them wanting to do things for you. There wasn't anything I could do. I was just there." He kissed her again.

"Me, too . . . me, too . . ." She said, her lips on his as she squeezed the words out of the corner of her mouth.

He released her and looked at her again. "Why don't we run away and get married?"

"Let's do . . . oh, Randy, let's do."

"Come on . . ." They got up and each started running in a

different direction. Then they stopped. "Your car or mine?" They laughed.

"I'll follow you, Randy . . . old Mac . . . I'll follow you anywhere."

"You'd better. Follow me to your house and leave your car."

"They'll catch us and stop us."

"We'll turn off the lights and slip into the driveway, then you get in my car."

They started running, but just before they got to Randy's car they slowed down and walked. Randy's arm was tight around Molaine. They didn't talk, they just walked. Then as they got to the car, before he opened the door for her, he said, "You won't feel bad if we don't have a temple marriage? We'll have to wait a year, you know, if we should run away tonight."

"I know. We've waited a long time and passed the tests."

"Yeah. Ever since I went through the temple before my mission I've visualized you across that alter. You know how many weddings I've attended waiting for us to be in that temple together?"

"How many?"

"Four. Four friends have married . . . bit the dust. Now, it's my turn." He tightened his hold on her, tucking her head under his chin as he kissed the top of her head. "Your hair smells like shampoo. Where's the perfume I gave you?"

"I never wear the perfume of the missing groom when I'm running away."

"Good, then we'll run away together."

"It would be fun, wouldn't it?" He lifted her chin and looked into her eyes. She nodded.

"Anything is fun with you. Randy, how could I have thought about leaving you?"

"Just don't ever do it again. And I'm going to make sure you don't. We're getting married tonight."

"At night?"

"Well, it might be morning before we get there. . ."

"And you are going to spend the night with me before we are married? Why, Elder McGregary, what will your moral code say?"

"I'm not taking any chances on losing you. I can't trust you, so I'll marry you."

"I'm so glad your intentions are honorable." She was teasing him the way she'd always teased him, and she felt good the way she always felt around Randy, ever since they were little. She'd had fights with him, but she always felt good, could tell him anything.

As they climbed in Randy's car and drove to the parking lot where Molaine's old family car waited, Randy stopped the car but didn't get out. They just sat there thinking quietly. Randy reached for her hand in the dark and held it tight.

"A fun dream, huh?"

"Running away?"

"Yeah. Not especially the running away, Molie . . . just the idea of being with you without anyone or any dress material or anything coming between us."

"It won't be long now, Randy. Mr. Mac, you are almost a married man."

"You promise?"

"I promise."

They were quiet a minute longer while he just squeezed her hand, tightening his fingers around her diamond. Then he lifted her hand, and the parking lot lights caught the sparkle.

"I spent two summers working for that ring."

"But I thought you just bought it."

"No. I've had that ring in a safe. I've been paying on it for almost three years. My uncle owned the jewelry store, and he gave me a no-pay extension while I was on my mission. I knew I'd need a ring someday."

"Oh, just for somebody, huh? Just any old girl?"

"Sure." She smiled, and he meant to hold out and tease her, but the light danced on her hair, and he couldn't resist. "I've known for a long time . . . it was always you."

"Then why were you running out?"

"I couldn't find you. I thought I could stand it, three months of preparation . . . but I couldn't find you in the middle of it all.

I'm always confused without you, Mo."

"I guess that's what's wrong with me, too." They were quiet again. Then Randy slipped his arm around her and pulled her over to his side.

"We can't do it, can we?"

She shook her head, and the tears began to slide down her face again.

"Mo, we can't give up all the rest of our dream, can we? The waiting, the living for the temple, the hurting our parents. . ."

She swallowed and shook her head again.

"We'll be all right now. We can wait for the wedding, can't we? Now that we've found each other again."

She nodded and sniffed. He handed her a handkerchief from his back pocket. She took it and wiped her eyes.

"I think that's why I fell in love with you."

"Because I'm good at waiting?"

"No." She sniffed and shook her head again. "Because you were the only boy I ever knew that carried a clean, white handkerchief."

"She's crazy, Elders. This girl I'm marrying is absolutely crazy. I shudder to think what the rest of my life will be, married to this crazy, cute girl." Then he stopped talking and looked at her. "I shudder to think what life would be like without you. Come on, future Mrs. McGregary. I'll put you in your car and follow you home. I've got to make sure you are safe, can't take any chances now." He got out, went around to her side of the car, and opened the door.

"Question," she said, pausing while he held the door.

"Question . . . go ahead."

"If you weren't looking for me tonight, what made you come to the steps?"

"I don't even know how I got there. I was just trying to think. You and I have done a lot of thinking walking up and down those steps through the years. I guess my inner self knew more than I did and just brought me here."

"Me, too. I guess we really aren't free agents after all; we're bound by what's smarter than we are."

"Come on . . . I'll follow you home."

"Randy?" She got out of the car, and he led her to the old family vehicle she'd driven into the parking lot.

"Yes?"

"I was just thinking. I guess my dad was worried about his car, thinking I might not bring it back."

"This old thing?"

"My dad likes this old car."

"Yeah, I get it. I guess he was worried about the car. But I don't suppose he gave you a thought. Fine responsible girl."

"I am responsible, Randy. I'll be a good wife, really I will, just as soon as I settle down."

"I don't care if you're responsible or not . . . I just love you."

"And Randy?"

"Yes?"

"You won't trust me anymore, will you? You'll call me everyday until we get married?"

"And then I won't have to call you again."

"Oh, Randy. I think I'm going to get mad at you again."

"And put another bump on my head?"

"It's called a lump . . . before we get this marriage on the way, you just might have a whole head of lumps."

"All the more for me to rub." He smiled and closed the car door, and she started the engine.

2

"I've got rice coming out of my ears." Randy slid into the car seat beside Molaine and started the car. They squealed out of the parking lot and were on their way.

"Where are you taking me, Randy?"

"To the moon, the stars, another planet, and be with you without any aunts or uncles or . . . ."

"It wasn't so bad, was it?"

He pulled her close. The feeling of her tight against his side made his throat hurt. She was so . . . so . . . there weren't any words to explain how he felt about her. From that moment only a few hours in the past, when they knelt across the alter in the temple, Molaine all in white, her eyes full of the beauty of eternity, her tender face and angelic look . . . how would he ever tell her all that and not sound like an idiot. They had cried together. They were happy, smiling, and they had cried. Not just a little tear, but tears of joy had rolled down both their faces, and he didn't even care if he didn't seem manly. He felt like a man now, more of a man than he had ever felt in his life. She was his, his to protect and take care of, to love and . . . .

"Well, was it so bad? All the fuss and . . . oh, Randy, did you hate it?"

"No, I loved it. I loved every aunt and uncle and cousin . . . I can't believe how much they did for us."

"I know. I have the most beautiful wedding gifts in the

world. And my showers. You wait until you see my personal frills. Everyone was so nice. Uncle Allen gave us a hundred-dollar check, did you know that?"

"You forgot to mention it. I've married a girl with rich relatives and does she ever have a lot of them!"

"I do, don't I?"

" 'I do, don't I?' What kind of grammar is that? Are you sure you went to college?"

"I never said no such thing; you is assuming things again, Mr. McGregary."

"I could be, Mrs. McGregary."

"It's true. I have that terrible name."

"What's so terrible? It goes with the territory."

"And the territory belongs to me."

"That it does." He leaned over and kissed her.

"Watch the road. Don't wreck our marriage before we get started."

"This marriage isn't going to be a wreck. It's a good one, solid, full of love. . ."

"I'm so glad you didn't mind the relatives."

"They go with the territory. Your mom was super and your dad . . . I think it was hard on him to give up his first daughter, but he didn't say anything. First thing in the morning let's find a floral and send some thank you's to a couple of good families, all right?"

"All right! Randy, I love you."

"You said that rather easily. Sounds nice. Did you stand my family?"

"I love them. I especially love your little sister, April. She cried tonight when we got ready to leave. Did you notice?"

"Yeah, she's my pal. She waits on me, you know. But that's all right, you can do it now."

"Wait on you? That will be the day."

"Remember the man said we should never refuse to do anything the other wants the other to do?"

"Now who hasn't been to college?"

"I shall attend later." He kissed her again, quickly. . . "Much later. Right now I've got to drive this car."

"Then do it." They drove in silence for a while, Molaine clinging to Randy's arm as if he might disappear if she let go. "Randy?"

"Yes, dear."

"Oh, Randy, you say that like we've been married a hundred years."

"I know, dear."

"Randy, will we do it?"

"Do what?"

"Will we always say our prayers together before we go to bed?"

"Of course. What did you think? Besides, that's what the man said, isn't it?"

"He was so good, wasn't he? I can't even remember his name, but I keep hearing his words go round and round in my mind. Randy, if we always have prayer, we'll have a wonderful life together, won't we?"

"We'll have the most wonderful life anybody ever had. I'm going to be rich, and you're already beautiful, so how can we lose?"

"I want to be as happy as this when I'm eighty years old."

"Are you going to get to be eighty years old?"

"Only if you'll stay with me."

"I'll be there."

"Randy, how far are we going tonight?"

"I can't tell you; it's a surprise."

"Surprise me now."

"I would, but I have to drive this car." He gave her a look that made her toes tickle.

"Elder Randy . . . what are you saying?"

"Just an ordinary statement any married man might make."

"I think I have a lot to learn about you, Randy."

"You are right. And we start tonight."

It was a beautiful honeymoon. Starting with a motel in the mountains, overlooking a lake, Randy and Molaine McGregary started their life together. All the dreams they had ever thought of seemed to roll into a whole week of happiness. And the hiking, swimming, movies, and food were enjoyed but not remembered. All they knew was the thrill of being together, doing things together, and looking forward to a future of all the things they'd been planning and living for all their lives. No disagreements, not one irritated word. It was heaven, and they both knew it but didn't dare talk about it. They just went on laughing. Yet, though she wasn't consciously aware of it, Molaine began to worry. One night, toward morning, as Randy turned over to put his arms around her, he found a wet pillow under her face.

"Molie?" He sat up quickly. "Molie, what's the matter? Do you hurt somewhere?" She shook her head. "Then what's the matter?" He reached for a tissue and wiped her nose and eyes.

"I don't know. It's all so wonderful. It seems so perfect. We are truly one, like we were one person. We think alike, feel together. It can't go on like this forever."

"Oh, honey, of course it can."

"No, people aren't this happy, not in this life. This is like dreaming of what eternity is going to be . . . like I'm in eternity now."

"Honey, don't cry. I feel the same way." He took her in his arms. "Don't worry, we'll have our problems."

"What kind of problems?"

"I don't know, things like . . . we'll have to go home and get to work. You'll have to go to work, and we'll have to register for school. My job won't let us live like this for long. And we can run out of money, too. In fact, we are down to our last twenty dollars."

"Then we'll have to go on a diet. You call those problems? It will be fun as long as we're together."

"Then why the tears? Come on, be happy . . . this is our life to live. Let's live it . . . live, live." He dramatically swept his arm in a circle. She threw a pillow at him, and he grabbed her by the feet as she tried to get out of bed and pulled her back. She pushed him off his side of the bed, and he ended the fight by carrying her into a cold shower. She let out a yell as the icy water ran over her, clothes and all, and she clung to him until they were both soaked and freezing.

Like two little friendly bears playing together, they were friends first and lovers next as the magic of love surrounded them, showing them the beauty of. life that only being in love could sponsor.

And then it was over, their stay in the mountain motel close to the lodge. They packed their bags just before noon.

"Are you sorry it's over, Mrs. McGregary?"

"Nope. I'm ready to go home."

"You don't like honeymooning with me?"

"I'm going to be honeymooning with you all my life. I'm anxious to get home and put all our lovely gifts away. We have so many to open that we haven't even seen yet."

"There's work waiting at home, not just playtime like this."

"Didn't I ever tell you? I like work. I want to shine my apartment and put up my pictures and cook for you. Sound dull?"

For an answer he reached across the bed and grabbed her.

"No, no, Husband, I've just finished combing my hair."

"Who cares?"

"I care. You want me to look like a mess? Everybody will feel sorry for you, married to . . . ."

"A mess? Sure, I don't care." He kissed her, and her arms encircled his neck to hold on tight.

They left the beautiful mountain lodge motel a little after noon, checking out just under the deadline. They drove along the mountain pass, fascinated with nature's picturesque paintings. It was just a few miles from the lodge as they were driving over the top of the hill when a car, unseen from their side of the road, swerved around a bend, weaving from the impact of taking the turn too fast. Randy instantly pulled onto the shoulder of the road. The car missed them, but the impact of their car wheels against the soft shoulder of the road made the edge give way, and their car turned over, rolling over three times before it hit the ravine below, right side up. The crash rang out over the hillside, and then there settled an unearthly silence.

"Molie . . . Molie . . ."

Molaine was faintly aware of her own name. Someone was calling her. "Yes . . . ."

"Come on, move a little, you've got to get out of the car." She tried to move and groaned with pain. She hurt all over. "Come on, Molie. You can do it. I'll help you. . ."

"Randy?" She tried to see him, but he was only a mist. "Randy?" And then she didn't hear anymore.

On the top of the hill a police car rounded the bend.

"Blackmore, it has to be along here somewhere. That's the rock I saw from the top of the hill."

"Are you sure, Officer Dunn? I didn't see anything."

"Just as we rounded the curve, I saw that car go over. Now slow down along here. There, look . . . the road edge is pushed over . . . and there, look, that has to be the car. It's still burning. Must have hit the gas tank."

"It's burning all right. There can't be any life left in that one."

As the officers climbed down into the ravine to examine what was left of the burning automobile, they found a man and a woman stretched out on the ground a few yards from the wreck.

"How did they get out of the car?"

"If they were thrown out, they wouldn't be lying there together like this," said Blackmore, leaning over the body of the woman. "She's still breathing. What have you got there?"

"He's breathing, too . . . I think. I'll radio for an ambulance."

"Do you suppose that car that was speeding uphill had anything to do with this?"

"Can't say, but the tracks on top should tell us something."

"I just can't figure how they got out. Look at the framework of that car. You'd have to be the Thin Man on a diet to get out of that thing."

"Only a miracle could get anybody out of there, and I don't see anybody by that name around. While I'm radioing, see if you can find any identification."

The lights of the operating room blazed over Randy's head. Molaine lay quietly in a white hospital bed just one story above.

She lay quietly as if dead, her color that of the white sheets beneath her head. She stirred and groaned a little. A nurse stepped to her side.

"Are you in any pain, Mrs. McGregary?"

"N-o . . . oh, I hurt. Randy . . . where's Randy?"

"Your husband? We'll know about him in a little while. He's alive. You've had an accident."

"Where am I?"

"In a hospital. Are you uncomfortable?"

"I feel like I've been run over by a truck. Can you tell me what happened?"

"The report is coming in. We only know you had an accident."

Molaine looked around the room through a haze. Then she drifted off again into a pool of nothingness, a wind in her ears. She could hear Randy's voice calling her again, the way she had heard it after the accident. It was the only thing she could remember. Then the wind went away, and she was aware of the hospital room again. "He called me before," she said half aloud.

"Did you say something?" The nurse stood beside her again.

"No, I'm all right. Don't let me sleep until I find out about Randy."

"You can sleep, Deary. I'll wake you when we have any news. You have to get well. Your husband will need you after this."

"My husband . . . he must be bad, or you'd know. Tell me, nurse, I want to know the worst and the best. Tell me." Molaine tried to sit up. The nurse restrained her. "There has to be more than you are telling me."

"Rest, please rest. I'll get the doctor."

"Yes. I want to talk to him."

She slipped off again into the pool that seemed to go down and down into darkness. The wind was in her ears again, but she held on, held on when there was nothing to hold to, only Randy's voice calling her as she had heard it after the accident came through. When she came to again, the doctor was there.

"Tell me, Doctor. What about Randy, what about my

husband? Just tell me the truth."

"All right, I'll tell you all we know at this point." The doctor sat beside her. "We are doing all we can for your husband. He has a broken arm and some broken ribs that are giving him trouble, but that's not our main concern. He is unconscious, and we aren't sure why . . . a blow . . . maybe his back. We're going to find out. That's all we know. I'll tell you whatever we find out. Does that help?"

"Yes, Doctor."

"We also let your parents know. You were both out when you came into the hospital, so we found your identification and called your home."

"Thank you. What about our family doctor, I mean . . ."

The doctor took her hand. "Of course, you can call anyone you wish, but we had to start finding out. Now you get some rest. You've had some banging up, too. However, your x-rays don't show any serious problems. You'll be uncomfortable and dizzy, and there may be other symptoms, but you should be well soon."

"I'm all right, Doctor. Take care of Randy. Please take care of Randy."

"Of course." She slipped back into the whirling wind in her ears again.

Molaine awoke in the night when the nurse and doctor were gone. The fuzziness in front of her eyes was gone, and she lay there, staring into the darkness of the room, facing the feeling inside her. There was a possibility she could lose Randy. She covered her face with her hands, trying to shut out the fears that gathered there.

How can I live without him? Or what if it is his back? What if he's crippled? Oh, please no. That can't be. I won't let it be. I'm a fighter, I'll fight. But she knew, for the first time in her life, that there are some things that fighting won't change. And if it did, if she should put her will against the Father's, and Randy should live, and that wasn't his mission . . . oh, her teachings of the Gospel and her understanding went deeper than she thought. She was suddenly aware that this great love, this happiness she knew, was not of her own making. Yes, she had kept herself clean and lived worthy, kept the rules of morality and been married the right way . . . oh yes . . . married the right way.

Suddenly the evening she had run away came back to her. She and Randy had wanted to be together so much that they almost ran away. They had been serious, and yet something inside wouldn't let them.

"Oh, Heavenly Father," she breathed, "thank you for keeping us on the track. What if we'd missed our beautiful temple wedding? And now, even if you should take Randy . . . oh please, don't, but if you should . . . I know we will be together sometime. Oh, yes, Heavenly Father, thank you for guiding us. But now . . ." Closing her eyes against the darkness of the room, she thought about Randy.

She had been with boys that were fun, boys that had accomplished more socially than Randy, but they hadn't meant anything. She hadn't known she was in love with Randy until after his mission, really. He'd just always been there, next door, been there when she needed a friend. What if he wasn't there?

"Oh, Father," she pled for help from the only source she knew that could help her now. "Take care of my Randy. He is so good. We have so many plans, don't let him leave me now, Father. I have just found him. Let us both live together to serve Thee, Father. I know you have the power to heal him or take him, and I don't want to tell you how to do your job or keep my Randy from anything you want to call him to do. But please bless us. If you will let us live together, I promise to dedicate my life to Thy service, Dear Father, and to the Gospel. With renewed energy I dedicate myself to the covenants we made in the temple only a few days ago. Oh, I know I shouldn't bargain, and if we must be separated . . . if we must, then I ask for strength. I will be obedient, Father. I will. But remember, Father, all those children we've dreamed of, the family we've planned. They need a father here on earth. Let Randy be their father, please."

She rolled over in bed, and there was a sharp pain in her arm. On through the night she talked to her unseen Father in Heaven while she reviewed in her mind the things she had learned in seminary and in church. They had been tested before, but this was a new test, a more difficult test, a new concept.

She had never felt so little, so helpless. She'd been born a fighter, but there wasn't anything to fight now, except the will to follow the feelings inside her, to want to be part of the plan of life. As she talked, she felt closer to her Heavenly Father than she had ever felt before. She had had prayers answered, but this was different. She didn't know how this prayer would be answered, yet she felt a peace she had never felt before.

Thoughts kept running through her mind. She talked and thought and prayed. She tossed and pleaded and hurt there in the dark. She completely faced the fact that life wasn't hers to take or give, that life here should be obedience to the will of the Father. She seemed to see all things in a new light. Life was service, as Christ had served, with or without Randy. There was a special feeling she had gained in her few short days with Randy, of loving wholly and being loved by a righteous man, a man of God, for Randy was a man of God and knew how to serve. And she knew in that moment, looking into the darkness of the room, that a light had been turned on in her life, and she would never be the same again. She had tasted real love, and she knew whatever happened she would never go back to being the way she was before. That was a good life, too, but so young, so immature, so empty in comparison to what she felt now. Randy had shown her a beauty that changed every concept she had ever had. And she had been taking it for granted.

"Father," she whispered into the darkness, "I will be a cheerful person, I will radiate the love I have known no matter what I have to go through. Father, I will do my very best. I promise." With a smile on her lips and a stronger faith in her heart, she fell asleep.

By morning, the crisis had passed, and there was news of Randy's condition.

"He has a fractured left arm, a crushed rib, and a lot of pulled ligaments in his back. He's waking up now. His medication is wearing off."

"When can I see him?"

"We'll get you into a shower first. After that, he should be ready for you. I'll go get your clothes."

"Have I any clothes?"

"The officers that found you brought in two bags. They found them when they went back to check the road marks. The trunk evidently burst open and threw them out when the car turned over and rolled down the hill."

"I can't believe that. The officers said the car was all burned."

"There were quite a few strange things the police haven't been able to figure out."

The nurse disappeared, and Molaine was left to wonder about the many miracles. Her nice wedding things had been saved. She wondered why? She shook her head in amazement and rolled over in her bed to say another prayer.

"Oh, thank you, Heavenly Father. Thank you. I'll try and take it from here."

Stiff and sore from scratches and bruises, still dizzy but out of danger, Molaine tried to make herself sit up. It was difficult but not too difficult; nothing would ever be too difficult again, she decided. She had Randy; he had survived, and they would be together again.

After her shower, she was brought in to see Randy.

"I'm so grateful you made it." Randy weakly reached for her hand. "I don't remember anything after I saw the car coming toward us."

"Then how did you get me out?"

"I didn't get you out. I thought you got me out."

"No. All I remember is your voice calling to me, telling me I had to get out. The police said you must have opened the door for yourself and then got me out, but they can't figure out how you did it with your broken arm. The space where you were sitting wasn't big enough for a baby, and yet . . . and I heard you call my name. I really did."

Randy didn't say anything, he just looked at her. She went to him. He put out his good arm, and they held each other tightly.

"We've had more than our share of miracles," he said softly.

3

Molaine put the yellow candle sticks in their silver holders and sat them on the table. She stood back and looked at her creation. It wasn't much of a table, but the dishes were nice—thank goodness for wedding gifts. The atmosphere had to be the best for sharing the wonderful news with Randy.

She went into the bedroom to change her clothes to her one good pair of lounging pajamas. She had to look glamorous tonight. It might be a long time before she would look this way again. Examining her image in the mirror, she looked at the front view and then the side view, shook her head, touched her ears with the last fourth-ounce of her best perfume, and, humming a tune, went to check dinner. Randy would be home any moment, and she wanted the kitchen to look pretty and smell good. The meat was just right. They couldn't afford meat often, and this meatloaf had to be the best. It just had to taste like steak.

She put the salad on the table, hoping it wouldn't be there long enough to wilt, and was just pouring the salad dressing into a china server when the telephone rang. With the dressing bottle still in one hand, she lifted the phone to her ear.

"Hello." It was Randy. Her heart did a little jumping. His voice sounded like an excuse. She could tell the minute he said her name.

"Mo, I'm going to be late in the lab tonight. We've got a

project here we can't put away yet. Don't wait up for me; you need some sleep."

"Oh, it's all right. I'll wait. I haven't seen you at all lately. I work and you work, and you go to school, and I work. I mean I miss you, Mr. Mac."

"I know, me, too. But you haven't been looking your in-the-pink self lately. Get some sleep."

"But you've got to eat. I've got dinner ready and. . ."

"Can't help it. Save it for tomorrow. Got to go, Mo. . ." There was a click, and Randy wasn't there anymore. Deflated, she wanted to sit down and cry.

"Darn!" She banged the salad dressing bottle down on the table. "He won't be home until midnight, I know him. I have to leave by 4:00 a.m. for work at the telephone company. I teach after that, and we won't even see each other for three days. A quick meal . . . no time to be romantic or to tell my news. . ."

She walked around the tiny apartment. It was just one room and a bath. The kitchen was shut up behind folding doors, and their bed came out of the wall. They'd had such a darling place after their honeymoon, but they'd only lived in it one month. The rent was a gift from Uncle Avery for one month. They'd thought they could keep the apartment while they finished school, but after the accident, with the car gone, the insurance only paying part, they'd had to give up the apartment, and Molaine had to give up school. She had to be happy with a few night classes.

"But what does it matter?" she said aloud as thoughts of the past came over her. "I can get my teaching certificate, eventually. Or, at least I could have, until . . ."

Molaine walked around again, viewed the kitchen and the food she had prepared so carefully. It wasn't like she had time to prepare this kind of meal every day. No, once in a while she got off early. This had been the first time in a week, and she'd planned tonight..

She put the salad in a crisper and turned off the oven. There wasn't much she could do about the meatloaf now.

When the kitchen was cleaned up, she sat down to study,

but her long hours with no sleep began to tell. Her eyes wouldn't stay awake for anything as quiet as studying. Getting up, she went to the old typewriter that had been with her through high school and sat down to compose a jingle.

> You didn't come home to hear my news,
> So a formal announcement I've decided to choose.
> A boy or girl I cannot say,
> But it's due about the middle of May.
> You might not know who wrote this letter,
> But that just might be all the better.
> I suppose that now it's up to you—
> It's obvious to me—but *you'll* have to
> GUESS WHO?

Laughing at herself, she fixed Randy a plate of food, put the note on top of the plate, and went to bed. How long she slept before Randy got home she wasn't sure, but her next consciousness was Randy's arms around her, his kiss behind her ear, his voice whispering to her.

"Guess who? Guess who?"

"Randy?"

"Right, Randy, Mr. Mac, your husband, and the father of our child. You crazy girl, why didn't you tell me?"

"Would you have come home in the middle of . . ."

"I'd have come home. I might have caused a lot of problems for a few late lab workers, but I'd have come home."

"Next time I'll get you home."

"Next time? Wait a minute. We are going to have these children one at a time, aren't we?"

"Who knows?" She smiled and tightened her arms around his neck.

He laughed and held her tight. "I can't afford you, woman. You are a luxury I just can't afford."

"And our baby. Will it be a luxury, too?"

"All good things are luxuries. I can't afford any of them." He kissed her, and she felt his excitement. When he stopped, she looked at him seriously.

"You're glad, aren't you, Randy?"

"Of course, I'm glad. That's our goal. Wife, family . . ."

"But you did want to wait."

"So? Someone wiser has made that decision. We'll be all right."

"You won't have to give up school?"

"The worst that can happen is that I might have to go a little longer."

"I don't want it to be longer."

"It will work out. Don't worry. It will work out." He snuggled up even closer to her. "How far along are you?"

"Just two months. I wanted to make sure."

"And you didn't tell the daddy? Isn't that illegal?"

"Nothing's illegal for a mother."

"You'd better not keep secrets from me. I like to know when I'm having a baby."

"I wish we could arrange for you to have it. You'd be famous."

"I'd rather you be famous, little mother. I think a lot about having children, but if I had to do the having . . . well, we wouldn't have many."

"I see what you mean. Well, darling, you might not make a very good mother, but I know you'll make a wonderful father."

"You, Mrs. Mac, are just prejudiced."

"I sure am. And I'm also a lover."

"Hmmmm . . ." He looked at her in the quiet of the moonlight that came through their tiny window.

"Well, Mr. Mac?"

"Hmmmm, I don't know. You'll have to prove it."

Picking up a pillow, she threw it at him. He grabbed for her, but she slipped away and ran into the living room. He ran after her, caught her, picked her up, and carried her back to bed.

"Mrs. Mac, you can't be running around the apartment at this time in the morning. What will the neighbors below think?"

"They'll think you're beating me. And in my condition, too."

He smiled at her with the old look that always melted her, his look of love, of goodness that made her always remember the depth of their love. Tears suddenly welled in her eyes, and a tingling pulsed through her toes. "Mr. Mac, your wife, the mother of your children, would like to be kissed."

He smiled and took her in his arms.

Antonette McGregary was born the last part of May, just after school was out. She was born on a beautiful morning, and by noon mother and daughter were doing fine. It hadn't been an easy birth, and Molaine had had a long, painful delivery. She was tiny in all the wrong places, and the doctor used a little surgery. When it was over, Molaine lay in her hospital bed, exhausted, without enough strength to lift her hand. As Randy leaned over to kiss her, she so wanted to touch his head, but she didn't have the strength to lift her arm.

"Thank you, Molie, thank you for a beautiful daughter."

"You're welcome," she said weakly and then passed into sleep.

The next time she awakened, it was to hold her baby. Randy had gone to work for a few hours but was now back.

"Isn't she beautiful, Randy? She's so little and soft and . . . is she really all ours?"

"That's what her hospital bracelet says. All ours. That is if I can get enough money to get her out of here."

"I'm sorry, Randy. I thought I'd have enough saved before she came but . . ."

"But you spent it on my schooling. I know. I'm the one that's sorry. But I'll make it up to you, honey. Thank you for Toni."

"Toni. Will we call her Toni?"

"If we don't, other people will. I can't see them saying Antonette, not today—it's too complicated. But I like Toni, don't you?"

"Toni is cute. She looks like a Toni, doesn't she?"

"Now how would we know? Have you ever seen a Toni?"

"Of course, right here in my arms with her tiny fingers holding tight to mine. This is the only Toni that matters from now on."

"Holding her baby and talking to Randy helped her to feel

better. She loved them both so much. "Randy, when can I go home?"

"As soon as you feel like it."

"I'll feel like it in the morning. Will we be able to raise the money?"

"I've got some ideas. I'll be back for you in the morning. Get some sleep so they won't keep you here."

Randy left Molaine and the baby when visiting hours were over, but he didn't go right home. He had some figuring to do. The extra job he'd taken when school was out hadn't brought in enough money to pay the hospital bill. He'd thought there might be time, if she went overdue, like some of their friends always did, but Molaine had come on her exact date, and he still didn't have the money. Somehow, he had to come up with it for the hospital by morning.

He walked around campus a while, and then knew he was only stalling. The only thing he could do was go to the bank. He called and made an appointment for his lunch hour. He spent a lot of time talking to the banker and found out there wasn't any way he could borrow the money without collateral, and they didn't think a baby was collateral. The only way he could get the loan was if his father signed with him. He hated to ask. He'd always made his own way. His parents had helped him while he was on his mission, but except for that, he had always taken care of himself. His parents didn't have much money, and they'd worked like dogs for what they did have. He didn't want to involve them in his financial affairs. But he had to get Molaine out of the hospital. He was already going to school on school loans, all they would lend him. He had no alternative but to swallow his pride and call his father.

Randy's father met him at the bank and signed the note that gave Randy enough money to get Molaine and little Toni out of the hospital. Before he left the bank, he said goodbye to his father, assuring him that it would all be paid back, that he wouldn't have to worry about it just because his signature was on the loan. His father had been very kind and sympathetic. But Randy was embarrassed. He stood there on the bank steps watching his father disappear down the street and made a vow within himself.

I'm a father, and I haven't got enough money to get my little daughter out of the hospital without borrowing. This will never happen to me again. I swear this won't happen to me again. I'll work night and day if I have to, and I'll learn to save money for emergencies. I'll put some aside, no matter how little, every payday. I will never be this broke again. I promise myself. I won't ever be this broke again. I'll be able to afford my children when I need to get them out of the hospital without having my father sign with me.

4

t wasn't an easy year, but it was a happy one. Molaine was often so tired she couldn't sleep, but she somehow managed to stay in school and work part-time at night, spending her days with Toni. Randy took over on his hours off while she got some sleep. She sandwiched in her studying while she nursed Toni.

"I've got to be the most talked about girl in school," Molaine related to Randy, as she studied for the few classes she still put into her schedule.

"What can anyone say about you, except that you're a woman crazy with ambition?"

"My friends think I'm old-fashioned."

"I think you're old-fashioned, too, and just a little crazy. But I'm stuck with you, an ordinary wife wouldn't fit into my schedule at all." He smiled, and Molaine turned up her nose and smiled at him.

"They think this nursing with my schedule is crazy."

"What do you think?"

"You know how I feel. Every time I give Toni a formula or start her on baby food she gets sick with a germ or an allergy. As long as I nurse her, she's great. But nursing is easier than standing over a sick bed, and Dr. Carson agrees that Toni is healthy and happy. He's a neat doctor. He says nursing has some advantages besides nutrition."

"What advantages?"

"He says mother's milk comes in such cute containers; it is always warm and up where the cats can't get at it."

"That dignified little doctor of yours said that?"

"I couldn't believe it. I'm sure I blushed, but he didn't seem to notice."

"Careful, I don't want any doctor getting familiar with my wife."

"A baby doctor?"

"Any kind of a doctor." He smiled, and she knew he was teasingly being jealous.

"I really like Dr. Carson. He's so cute with Toni. I'm going to hate moving away from him."

"Better prepare yourself; we're almost there. Graduation is coming up."

"I'm ready. Believe me, Mr. Mac, I'm ready."

"For what?" He laughed at her.

"To be the wife of a rich businessman."

"I've got to be rich now?"

"Of course. We have to afford all our children and go on a mission and . . ."

"Wait a minute. Let's get a job first." Randy put his head back in the book he was studying. Molaine was thoughtful, looking around their small apartment.

"You know, Mr. Mac, it's a good thing I haven't had a big house to take care of. I'd never have made it this far. But still, I haven't finished yet, and that worries me."

"What worries you?"

"I won't have my teaching degree when you graduate. I won't graduate with you."

"You've done all right, little lady. You're a wife, a mother, a housekeeper, a career girl . . . don't put yourself down. You've done more in all your fields than most women ever do."

"I've been blessed, Randy." She was suddenly serious. "But I promised myself I'd get that teaching degree to prepare myself."

"Prepare yourself for what?"

"Making a living if I need to, if anything happens to you."

"Nothing is going to happen to me. I was miraculously saved, remember?"

"But for how long? Anyway, in the economy of today most wives have to work at least part-time. If I can teach, I won't ever have to leave my children."

"Don't worry, you'll get it. I'll work it out with my new job, and you can finish."

"I don't know if the children will wait."

"What children?"

"Our six children."

"Are we still having six children?"

"Isn't that what you always said you wanted?"

"That's what I said, but I thought a year like this would discourage you."

"Not me. I'm not going to be the one to keep our children waiting up there. We'll have them as fast as we can manage. I'd almost like to get them all here at once, get the whole thing over with, and our kids on their way."

"Not in this one-room house, thanks anyway."

"No, I guess they'll just have to wait until you get some more money. Randy, I want a big house. I want to fill it with children."

"No wonder your friends say you are old-fashioned."

"I know. But look how blessed we are. It was hard to get the money for Toni, and we're still paying it back, but the greatest value for any money spent is a child. Don't you think?"

"She's an angel, all right. Well, that is most of the time," said Randy, still smiling as he started to read again.

They studied in silence a while, but Molaine's mind wouldn't stay on the papers in front of her.

"Which job do you think you'll take, Randy? I mean, you have those three offers; which one do you want?"

"I've thought about it so much I can't think anymore. I've prayed like crazy and investigated, but I guess when we get down to the wire, only the Spirit can tell us."

And that's the way it was. When Randy graduated, they

took the jobs one at a time, and together they prayed about them. Then, they discussed how they felt the next day.

"It looks like it will be the Western oil firm, doesn't it, Molie?"

"It's the one I feel good about, even though I thought it would be fun to go to Washington."

"Maybe that's not best for our family. How about a date to go to the temple in the morning?"

"Sure. It's a date. If I can get a baby sitter."

"Try April again."

"Maybe you haven't noticed, Mr. Mac, but your sister April is growing up and is beginning to date. I don't think she's going to be a baby tender for us too often anymore."

"One of these days you'll be able to afford to pay a baby tender, and then you can get one any time you want one. But you need to be with your husband sometimes. What about me?"

"I'll get a baby tender. We're doing it again, huh?"

"What do you mean?"

"You always ask for a date to go to the temple when you have a big decision to make."

"You figured that out, too?"

"Sure, a long time ago."

"Just going to the temple, to sit there quietly in that Godly place, makes me think better."

"Me, too." She smiled. "I just wanted you to admit it. Now let's discuss this job idea a bit more."

"What do you want to say about it?"

"Which one really interests you the most?"

"The job in California looks the best, pays the best, but it may not be right."

"It might be scary moving away from the folks, too. They've been so great to help us."

"We should learn to be on our own. I know we don't ask for their help much, but we need to know what it's like to be alone."

"I didn't know you felt that way about my parents."

"It's just that we have more opinions than we need sometimes."

"If you resent my parents, why don't you say so?"

"I love your parents."

"Yes, but you're always saying I should think for myself. I do think for myself, Randy. I just need somebody to talk to."

"You can talk to me, can't you?"

"Sometimes! But not all the time. Sometimes you're too involved in school to care about me or Toni. I go everywhere alone lately!"

"What can I do? This was finals week."

"I'm not complaining, but you need to understand that I need to talk to somebody, too. I don't want you to resent my relationship with Mother and Dad. You can talk to the guys; I don't have anybody. Well, the girls, but what do they know about me? Their problems are so different . . . guys, dates . . . we don't have very many married friends, and when you're talking to the guys, you leave me out."

"Honey, even though you're smart, you're not exactly an expert on scientific things."

"Well, if I don't finish school, you'll always think I'm too stupid to talk to. When I quit work and get my degree and read some books . . ."

"You don't have to do all that."

"Yes, I do. No matter what you say, I made a promise to myself, and I have to get my degree."

"Well, don't get uptight about it now."

"I'm not uptight, Randy. I pride myself in being calm, and you say I'm uptight."

"You're tired, Molie. Go take a nap with Toni."

"You sound like my father, sending me to bed." She laughed at the idea, but there was a note of irritation in her voice.

"I'm your husband sending you to bed. You need some rest."

"If I just didn't have to work."

"I thought you liked your job."

"What do you want me to say? We need the money."

"I haven't been a very good provider. That's what you're trying to say, isn't it? Give me a chance, and you'll see."

Emotion pulling at her, Molaine ran from the room, into the

hall where Toni was sleeping. She almost slammed the door behind herself, then remembered and shut it quietly. She wanted to cry for no reason at all; she just wanted to cry.

Randy stood alone, watching the door close behind her. He walked around a little, tried to study, but couldn't keep his mind on his work.

This wasn't like Molaine. She didn't usually get her feelings hurt over nothing. She didn't usually care when they had differences about their parents. She usually just laughed it off. The only time she was ever irritable at all, over little things, was when she. . . Randy snapped his fingers and went to tap on the door.

"Molie, come out. I need to talk to you."

He waited, and soon the door opened, and Molaine came out, tear-stained. Randy held out his arms, and she went to him, putting her head on his chest.

"I'm sorry, Randy. I don't know what's the matter with me. I'm just not myself lately."

"He put his arms around her to comfort her and said against her hair, "It's all right. You have a right to feel this way. It's very legal in the face of the coming situation."

"What situation?" She lifted a tear-stained face to look at him.

"Honey, have you been wanting strawberries lately? Or pickles? Or would you like me to find that little country market and get you some fresh-squeezed cranberry and apple juice?"

Her mouth flew wide open. "Randy, we're not . . ."

"Yes, honey, I think we're pregnant again. You can have the test to make sure, but I think we are pregnant."

"Oh, Randy. What will we do?"

"We'll have a baby, of course. Maybe this time it will be a boy."

"Randy . . . but I'll never get my teaching certificate now. I could barely make it with Toni. Oh, Randy, are you right?"

"Of course, I'm right. There's no other explanation."

"Explanation for what?"

"For you being irritable. Molie, I've seen you through every kind of crisis, and you are a most mature, controlled person, except . . ."

"Except when I'm sick and pregnant. Randy, what will I do?"

"You'll know what to do. You're the one that ordered six children."

"Only me? Not you?" Her voice was irritated again. Randy held up his hands.

"Me, too . . . don't get your feelings hurt. We're going to have to be careful with you for a few months."

She started to cry. "Randy, am I so terrible to live with?"

"Not for me. You're the only woman in the world for me, even with six children. We'll have fun raising them. Just think, this time you won't be in a one-room-and-a-bath apartment.

"Randy, you may not be right. I might not want you to be right for a little while, but if you are . . . Randy, I do want a little boy."

5

But their second baby wasn't a boy. She was another girl with lovely smooth skin. Randy was the first to hold her. After delivery he took her to the nursery in the hospital from the delivery room. The nurses, still busy cleaning up the delivery room, gave Randy an opportunity to be the first to sterilize himself and introduce their second daughter to her mother. And though Molaine was still glassy eyed, she managed a weak, happy smile, and Randy knew she understood. He was also on hand for the first feeding time.

"Aren't you bending the rules?" Molaine asked, lying on her hospital bed.

"Sure am. We have a few advantages in a small town. You're looking pretty all right for a mother of a new baby."

"I'm fine. Just hand me my baby girl."

"You seem to remember I told you she wasn't a boy. I wasn't sure you heard."

"I heard." She reached for the baby. "You were the one who who wanted a boy. I always wanted another girl."

"If she were triplets, you'd always want them, too, wouldn't you?"

"Of course. Our children are my children and worth all they cost."

"And she cost. But at least this time we didn't have to

borrow money."

"And we live in a three-bedroom house, like you promised, with room for the children. Isn't she beautiful, Mr. Mac?"

Randy pulled a chair up close and touched his daughter's face with his finger. "She is beautiful. Feel her skin. Just like velvet."

"Velvet . . . little velvet, your daddy likes you."

"Have you named her already?"

"What?"

"Velvet. You called her Velvet."

"Well, you said her skin was like velvet, so I just called her . . . well, we haven't a list of girls' names. You only made a list for boys."

"Velvet. I like it. Let's name her Velvet."

"Are you serious?"

"Of course, Molie. Velvet McGregary. That is a long enough name for any child. We can call her Vel. What do you say?"

Molaine smiled. "Whatever you like. I don't know, maybe it will grow on me."

"Just like the cows and chickens?"

She nodded. "Just like the cows and chickens. A college graduate and we're still stuck out here away from town and education."

"I beg your pardon; we have a good school only a bus away. You have done very well with your home study, and you don't have to work."

"Work? I spend more hours keeping the house and animals and teaching piano than I used to spend at work."

"I thought you liked it."

"I do. I feel free and happy and love my job with the youth, but they all need so much, and I have so little to give."

"You give all you have, Molie. You do a good job with the kids. It's been a good eight months. Don't you think? We've accomplished a lot."

"You've accomplished a lot. You have the best group of scouts in the territory, you make good money with the oil company, and I don't see you long enough to pick a fight."

"What can be better than that?" He leaned over and kissed her. "Thanks for another lovely daughter."

"You're welcome." Molaine uncovered her baby and began to look at her feet and knees.

"You're checking ten toes, right? Well, don't bother; I checked her all out, even before she had her first bath. She's perfect."

"How's Toni?"

"Took her to Sally's. She'll keep her until your mother gets here, unless you want her home."

"Sally is a good neighbor. I don't know what I'd do without her. What would I have done if she hadn't been home when I had to get to the hospital?"

"I'm sorry. I'm embarrassed that I didn't make it from work in time. But I got here before she was born. That makes me her legal father, doesn't it?"

"I guess you can't get out of that." Molaine reached for Randy's hand, and he held it tight.

"We've had a lot of blessings, Molie. This delivery wasn't so hard, was it?"

"Like a breeze. I feel wonderful. If it's always this easy, I wouldn't mind having my six right away."

"Even without your degree?"

"Do I really talk about my degree that much? Don't worry, Randy, I'm happy. I've never been so happy. Can you get me home by morning?"

Molaine arrived home the next day with Randy beside her to carry little Velvet in. She took a deep breath as he put her suitcase down, carried Velvet to her baby bed in her own room, and went to put the car in the garage. Molaine looked around. The house was so clean. And in the center of the table with a bouquet of flowers picked from garden was a note. Molaine reached for it. It was from Randy.

"Darling, (he only called her darling in letters and notes) I haven't much to offer in return for what you've given me today, except a clean house and all my love. Randy."

Moldine folded the note and wiped the sudden moisture from her eyes and was smiling when Randy came in. As he came close, she reached up with both her arms, and he held her close.

"Randy, I love you. As much as you have to do to take time to clean the house. You didn't have to, but I love you for it."

"It's all right. But if I ever do it again, I'll buy a dishwasher."

"Then I'll see that you get a chance right away."

"Woman, don't push your favors." Stooping over, he scooped her up in his arms. "It's time for you to get back to bed." She protested, but he carried her into their bedroom and put her on the bed.

"You made the bed with lumps in it."

"No complaints. At least I made it."

"At least you did. When do I get to see Toni?"

"Can't you wait until your mother comes?"

"She won't get here until tomorrow. I want to see Toni now. Besides, I feel great."

"Don't get up too fast. That was one thing the doctor warned me of. Be careful of drafts and remember your body has been through a shock even if you do feel good."

"You sound like a doctor."

"I may become one . . . at the rate they make money. I'll get Toni. Sally said she could come over if we need her. What do you think?"

"I'll manage with you and Toni. I haven't seen you for sometime, you know?"

"I know. We'll have today and then . . ."

"Then you've got to go out of town again?"

"Some problems in the field. I won't be long. The big boss wants to see me. Could mean a promotion."

"And more money?"

"Why, Honey, I think you're getting commercial."

"I have to be commercial now, with four mouths to feed and two bottoms to diaper."

"Maybe we'll get a raise. Would that help? And maybe the raise will mean relocation."

"I'll take the raise. I don't want to move again."

"If the company says go, we'll have to go or give up the job."

"After all I've been through to learn about cows and chickens."

"It's been a good move, hasn't it, Molie?"

"Yes, Mr. Mac . . . a rest from city life. The people are so good, and they band together and do things. We've been through a lot of troubles with people here. It would be sad to leave now, wouldn't it?"

"I'd hate to leave my boys. I think Gary's parents are about ready to come into the Church. That will be a happy day for Gary. He's been praying about his parents for a long time."

"You've done that, just loving those boys. Gary's father, like all the other scouts' fathers, thinks you are Mr. Wonderful, himself. And I agree—until you leave and go out of town again."

"Mike up your mind . . . hold your hand or make you money?"

"Well, since you put it that way."

Randy left the next morning, a few hours before Molaine's mother arrived. Sally went to the bus to meet Molaine's mother and bring her home. The minute her mother arrived, the questions, just hinted at in letters, began to come to light.

"Molaine, I can't see why you ever took this job, way out here in this little town, when you could have had your choice of so many others?"

"Very temporary, Mother. Basic training for the job Randy really wants. He has to take all the moves and do what the boss says, and then when he gets enough seniority, he can name his own place to live and stay there."

"But why this job?"

"We don't know. We just felt good about this one after we put it to the prayer test. We felt good about this one, and we didn't feel good about the others. That's it. There are some disadvantages."

"Some?"

"Yes, some. I don't really like it here. The climate is too cold, shopping too far away. But Randy has freedom to be creative, to do his own thing, more than he would have had in any of the other jobs. He's happy here. We're learning a lot. Isn't that what it's all about? Learning? At least when he is home, after he's through with the animals and inside for the night, he's all mine. I don't have to share him with the books I used to share him with."

"But why the farm . . . the cows and chickens?"

"I told you in my letters."

"I know, but it wasn't so real then. I didn't see it."

"It was this place or nothing. Mr. Grant, who owns this place, is principal at the high school. He's taking a leave this year and had to have someone to take care of his place. We needed a place to live . . . simple. You know Randy; nothing is too hard if the price is right, and this price was right. Besides, Randy always wanted to live on a farm. He used to visit his uncle's farm every summer."

"What about you? I don't see much growth or development or rest for you."

"Growth? Oh, yes, I'm learning things I never dreamed I'd learn." She laughed. "And development? Well, Mr. Grant arranged a course of home study that goes with the rent."

"With the rent?"

"Just kidding, but he did show me how to arrange my course of study so I can be studying some classes that will apply toward my teaching certificate."

"Are you still thinking about school?"

"Of course. I want my degree. For some reason it is very important to me. Oh, not that I get it now or next year or even the year after that, but I want to graduate even if it is with my sixth child. And rest? Well, who wants to rest? I want to go and go . . ."

"But you don't know anything about taking care of cattle or chickens or, or anything outside the house."

"I know, Mother, but I'm learning. Besides, Randy does it all. He's never gone very long, and when he is, there's George. He's a neighbor boy about a mile away. He takes care of the animals before and after school. It's fine, really, Mother. You'll love the quiet."

"No fire engines . . . I just might get used to it."

Molaine looked at her mother and reached out for her hand. Her mother came to sit on the bed beside her. There was a closeness they'd missed, a closeness they'd both missed since her wedding.

"Don't worry, Mother. It's all right. It's home! Anywhere with Randy is home."

"Of course, it is, dear. I'd better check Velvet again. She's pretty tiny to be left alone in her bed."

Molaine watched as her mother got up to leave and stopped her by the door. "Mother?" Her mother turned to look at her. "And Mother, there's another reason, too."

"Yes?"

"There is a little group of guys that needed Randy right now. He's doing wonders with them. They are starry-eyed doing the projects that Randy thinks of for them. These little guys have never had a challenge of anything different than cowboys and manure. Randy has them building boats, learning to shoot . . ." Suddenly Molaine's eyes filled with tears. "I guess the little guys are the main reason we came. Not that I'm not busy. I've got a group of Mia Maids that keep me standing tall . . . the Church keeps us active. . ." She stopped talking and just sat there looking at her mother. "There isn't any way to explain. I just know inside that we were supposed to come here. I'm not sorry."

Her mother smiled. "No need to explain—church activity and the Lord's callings. I've been answering those calls all my life, and the ones I wanted the least taught me the most."

"Something like that, Mother."

"I don't know why I asked. I've always trusted you. Besides," she threw up her arms easily, "mine not to wonder why, mine but to do or die. I'm here to help, and I'd better check little Velvet."

Her mother reappeared a few moments later. "She's sleeping like an angel. Shall I fix some lunch for you three girls?"

"We are three girls, aren't we, Mother. Four girls with you. Four girls and three generations. I must remember to take some pictures."

Out of the quiet, suddenly the silence was filled with long,

low moo's from a cow close by.   Toni woke up crying, and
Molaine ran to the window to look out.

"Molaine, that sounds very close. Do you have your cows
under your window?"

"No, we don't, Mother." One look and Molaine grabbed her
robe. "Mother, the cows are in the vegetable garden. They'll ruin
the whole thing. Take care of Toni, Mother."

"Molie, you can't be serious. You aren't going out. You're
still weak. Tell me what to do. I'll do it."

"I don't know what to tell you. I've got to decide when I get
there. This would happen while Randy is gone. And George.
Where's George? In school, of course. Call Sally for me. Her
number is on the phone book, right on the front."

"But Molie, wouldn't it be better to let the garden go?"

"Go?" Molaine turned at the door. "Mother, I spent all
summer helping Randy with that garden. I've been waiting for
fresh vegetables, and I'm not going to give them up. Besides, the
cows have to be put back in. If we lose the cows, we'd never get
through paying for them. Just call Sally; she'll know what to do."

That was the beginning. Molaine chased the cows, and the
little bull chased Molaine. She'd just get part of them out, and the
others would come back in while she was trying to fix a pole in
the fence. She was exhausted, discouraged, and ready to cry
when Sally got to her. Together, they finished the job. Sally
leaned a pole in the gap where they'd escaped and tucked the
wire over it. Molaine started to shiver.

"That should hold them until George gets here after school.
Let's get you back to bed." Sally looked at Molaine standing there
shivering. "Mo, are you crying?"

"No. I should be crying, but right now I'm so mad I just want
to throw things. If I had Randy here right now, I'd kill him. He
knew that fence needed fixing. He just didn't do it."

"But you're shivering."

"I know, I can't seem to stop."

"Mo, come on, we're going to get your feet in some hot
water."

"I'm all right, Sally. I'll warm up. I don't know why I'm

shivering. It isn't that cold out here. I've just been cold since I got home from the hospital, that's all." The shivering was so bad now she could hardly talk.

"Mo, you have what is commonly known as breast fever. It's the sickiest sick there is."

"Breast fever? What's that?"

"It's cold in your breasts, caking the milk. As weak as you are, all it takes is a little draft, and you've got it. I should know, I have it with every baby. Don't worry; we'll get your feet into hot water, some hot soup down you, and . . . Mo, don't faint, I've got to get you into the house."

That was the beginning but not the end. Mo shook and then sweat and shook again. Sally seemed to know just what to do until they got hold of the doctor.

"She's bad," Sally said to Molaine's mother, Muriel, in private while Molaine sat with her feet in hot water, the chills subsiding. "She needs to keep the milk flowing. Wrap her in some towels, loosely, if she wants to keep the milk. It may turn the baby's bowel movements green, but it will be all right. I've nursed mine through this stuff. The doctor might want to talk her into going to the bottle and giving her pills. But I don't do that. She'll be all right. It's just that she feels so sick. You always want to die for a few hours. Then you're all right again. She just can't get any drafts on her breasts. Once you've had it, the second time comes on faster. I'll be back in the morning."

"Randy . . ." whispered Molaine when her mother went to her. "Randy, I hate those cows."

"He isn't here, dear." Her mother thought she was a little delirious and didn't know what she was saying. With a dish of hot soup, she sat down beside Molaine and tried to get her to eat. "Here, dear."

"Randy . . ."

"He'll be back soon, dear."

"I know. He'd better get back soon, or I'll shoot those cows, and we'll spend the rest of our life paying for them."

"In the meantime we'll let someone else chase them, all right?"

"Mother?" she said weakly, "do you know that cows are more expensive than having babies in this place?"

6

Before Randolph Norman, first boy and heir to the McGregary name, was born Randy had been transferred three times, and they'd had a little taste of a lot of styles of living.

On the last move, while they were expecting baby Randy, Molaine found out what a long period of time three weeks could be. Randy had to go ahead to start his job and leave Molaine to come later—three weeks later.

"I love my children, but alone with the girls isn't my idea of living," Molaine complained to Randy on the telephone.

"I'll trade you places. I can't believe how still the quiet can be or how much I miss all the noise. I've found a house if you like it."

"A nice house? Oh, Randy, those words are my personal music. I'm leaving here and coming to you as fast as I can."

"Not too fast. Remember your condition. As long as we're having babies, let's have healthy ones."

"I'll remember. But I'm on my way."

"The company is sending a moving van. I can come home at the end of the week, or you can come now if you're ready, and we'll let the movers do the work."

"They can do the lifting, I'll do the bossing. I don't want anything broken this time. One more move, and we'll be out of china from our wedding."

And so, as the final days of her pregnancy came into view, they were a family again, living in a better house than they had ever had before, and were the proud owners of two cars. The big car was for Randy to travel in, that the company provided, and the little station wagon was Molaine's, that she had equipped with seat belts to strap the children in when she did her shopping.

Molaine waited and thought the last few weeks would never end.

"I'm too big to get under the steering wheel and too uncoordinated to drive. I just creep along. I'm too out of shape to buy a new dress, and I hate all my old ones."

"It won't be long now, Molie. And you don't look that big. You look beautiful."

"Randy, how can I get mad at you when you say such nice things?"

"Do you want to get mad at me?"

"Yes, I do."

"Go ahead, get mad. You've earned the right, now use it. What are we mad at?"

"You aren't mad. I'm mad. At least I'm very, very angry. My mother always said only dogs and crazy people go mad. The word is angry. So that's what I am . . . I'm angry. I'm filled with righteous indignation."

"Get it out. I'll straighten my shoulders and let the troubles rest there. That's what my mother always said. 'Randy, my boy,' she would say, 'you need strong shoulders to lift your burdens.'"

"Mr. Mac, are you laughing at me? Worse, are you making fun of me?"

"Not guilty. I'm just telling you what my mother said. You always tell me what your mother said, so I just want you to know that I have a mother, too."

"But my mother really said the things I tell you about."

"I know," he nodded. "So does mine."

"Randy, you idiot. Be serious. I really am mad at you."

"Back to mad. All right. Tell me why. Or should I ask?"

"Because you're going out of town again, and you know the minute you leave I'll have this baby."

"But I've waited all week, and you didn't do a thing. The doctor says another week at least. Don't worry, I'll be back."

"And if you aren't?"

"Molie, you just have to learn to do things on schedule. Now where would I be in my job if I just did things when I took a fancy. Schedule, my dear woman . . . you can have your baby the minute I get back."

"But what if your baby won't wait? What if you don't get back?"

"You can call the Bishop and his wife. They offered to help last Sunday, remember? Don't worry, I've made all the arrangements. But I intend to be here. Your doctor said I could stay right with you."

"I do wish you would."

Changing his smile, he was suddenly tender. He took her hand in his and lifted her chin. "You're frightened, aren't you?"

She nodded.

"Every birth takes a little more out of us, doesn't it? Fear, hurts, uncertainty . . . I wonder why we keep wanting more children?"

Looking up at his serious face, the tenderness in his eyes, tears suddenly blurred her vision. "It takes a little more, but we get so much more." She repeated his version of the television advertisement. He smiled.

"That's my girl." He kissed her. "Don't worry, everything is going to be all right. And you need more money, don't you?"

She nodded, and the tears spilled down her face, but she was smiling.

"I'll call every night and twice on Sunday."

"Sunday? You aren't staying until Sunday?"

"Not really, just another saying of my mother's."

"Randy, I could kill you for scaring me."

"Then the baby wouldn't have a father. Be careful what you say, or I might be found missing in a ditch somewhere, and you would be the suspect."

She sniffed and laughed. "It's so hard to be mad at you."

"Angry. And that's the idea." He lifted her chin again. "We'll have this baby, don't you worry. Unless you don't want to go through with it."

"Through with what?"

"The delivery."

Lifting her fist she hit him on the chest. "Randy, I will, I will, someday I'll kill you dead."

He shook his head. "You're smiling, but that's still a reckless saying."

"Well, just look at me, a big blimp, and you ask me if I want to go through with this."

"Just a thought. Your last chance of getting out of it."

"Randy," she said, being serious, leaning on him, tucking her head under his chin. "I do hate to bother other people. I'll be all right. I'll wait for you to get back."

"Don't take any chances. Your sister hated to bother people, too, including her husband, so she had her baby in the taxi."

"Randy, don't you dare bring that up now. If I did that, I would just die."

"I hope not. That would make it even worse for the baby. Born in a taxi and no mother."

"Randy, be serious. The doctor said not to be too far away."

"Last time it took you sixteen hours, and Velvet only weighed five pounds thirteen ounces. I can get back in three hours, one hour by plane."

"Take a plane. Really, Randy, I'm bigger this time, and I just have a feeling."

"You don't look bigger."

"You're just saying that to make me feel better."

"Well, do you feel better?"

"Yes. Now if you just wouldn't go away."

"I'll be back before you know it and with more money. I'm making better money because I take more responsibility. Until I get a business of my own, this is the best thing to do. You do like money, don't you? I wouldn't go if the doctor said there was any danger. Mostly I just hate being away from you. I could drop all responsibility and just be with you. But, Honey, there's a price for loving and children . . . enough money to take care of them, along with everything else."

"I know, Randy. I'm just being temperamental. I get to when I'm having a baby, right?"

So Randy left on his job and called every night. Nothing happened until his last call.

"All right, Molaine. I'm driving home, and I'll be there in a few hours."

"That's fine. Good you didn't have to fly and leave your car there."

"You're a good girl, right on schedule. But start thinking about having that baby. We'll go right to the hospital when I get back."

Only minutes after Randy had started home, Molaine started her labor, and things went fast. She called the Bishop and his wife, and they weren't home, so she called a neighbor to watch the children and drove herself to the hospital, arriving just in time. They rushed her to the labor room and didn't get to use the delivery room.

"It was wonderful," she said to Randy. "After two little baby girls that took me hours to deliver, we have a son, a big boy, and it was so easy."

"You didn't wait, Molie. I almost missed the whole thing."

"You made it for the final hour. That's your job, Mr. Mac. I'm glad we've got our son, Randy. Let's name him Randolph, just like his father, even if he does have to have a college education to spell his name."

"And his mother's maiden name, Norman, to keep the records straight, my Molie."

"All right. I guess we can call him Norm to keep both of you straight when I call you both to dinner at once."

"Just think, Molie, we have a son, a son at last. Not that I mind having two girls first. I always thought I wanted a house full of girls so that I'd be free just to love and spoil them. With a boy, I'll need to be an example image. With girls, I just have to be a love and money image."

"I think I understand all that, but right now he's just a baby and all mine, to love and dress and feed and take care of. Randy,

I'm so happy."

"When you're happy, that makes two of us."

"Randy, he's our biggest baby and my easiest delivery. How blessed we are. To be serious in this dizzying happiness, we've had more than our share of miracles."

"It's the life you lead, Molie. Not every woman can handle what you've been through in the past few years."

"Oh, Randy, I do hope it will last."

"The problems? I'm sure we'll have our share."

"No, the happiness, Mr. Mac. This wonderful, wonderful happiness. Are the girls all right at home? Are they happy? Do they miss me?"

"One question at a time. You can judge all the answers tomorrow when you come home."

"I can't wait. I always feel like it's all make-believe until I get home with you and the girls. I don't really like hospitals. And I have a strange feeling I can't explain."

"You're not getting one of your warnings again, are you? Honey, you've got to learn to take the good with the bad." He looked so serious, and his words were so funny Molaine laughed.

"Come and get me early. I'm sure I can go home tomorrow. I feel so great. It pays to have a fast delivery. I waited so long at home, I thought I'd never get to the hospital, but it was worth it. Our Randolph was ready to make his appearance, and he didn't do any waiting around. Just one shot, to ease the last minute pain, and here I am, back in my room, feeling like eating. And food tastes so good. Water tastes good, too. Randy, do you know water tastes good?"

"No. I've been drinking it for a number of years but no, I didn't know it tasted so good."

"Stop teasing. It tastes wonderful. You don't know. You've never been pregnant."

"No, I haven't. That's one experience I haven't had."

"But water . . . all the time I was pregnant it tasted so tasteless, like food and everything . . . a brown taste. Then suddenly I'm feeling wonderful, and water tastes so good."

"You drink all the water you want. That's one thing I think

we can afford."

"Thank you, Randy." Molaine lay back on her bed, and suddenly her eyes were tired. It was like she'd been on drugs, and they suddenly had worn off, leaving her exhausted. Sleep was settling over her. "Take good care of the girls, Randy. Tell them they have a little brother."

"I will. Get some rest. I'll be back in the morning. Everything is going to be all right."

Randy left Molaine quietly sleeping. He walked down the hall of the hospital and out into the night and didn't know that everything wasn't all right. He thought the funny feeling inside him was only the hurt he always felt when he had to leave Molaine.

Not tonight, he thought as he started a soft little whistle. *Tonight I'm a father for the third time, and this time I've got a son. A son! I guess every man wants a son sooner or later.*

But as he walked toward his car the funny feeling hit him again, and he thought about turning back to see if Molaine was really all right. Then he laughed at himself and climbed inside his car and drove home to tell his little girls they had a new baby brother.

7

"**R**andy!" Molaine called the next morning just before before Randy left for work.

"Calm down, Molie. What's the matter?"

"How can you ask me to be calm without knowing I'm upset? I haven't said I was upset."

"Molie, it's in your voice, just the way you can't keep lies out of your eyes. What's the matter?"

"Randy, I haven't seen Little Randy all night or even this morning. I've asked the nurses to bring him to me. The babies have been in with the mothers twice, but they haven't brought me our little Randy Norman. Something's wrong, I know something is wrong."

"Molie, settle down. I saw little Randy last night, and he was fine."

"But something must have happened; something is wrong, or they would bring him to me."

"What did the nurse say when you asked her to bring him in?"

"The night nurse said he woke up early and was hungry so they fed him in the nursery. It isn't normal, Randy. They always bring the babies in, even if they're asleep."

"Maybe they've changed things since the last time you had a baby."

"Randy, the women around me have babies, and they

haven't changed things for them."

"Still, that doesn't mean anything."

"Randy, I'm frightened. My stomach hurts, and you know when my stomach hurts, there's something wrong."

"I know, the mother instinct." Randy tried to calm Molie but remembered his own feelings.

"Randy, you believe me, don't you? Something has to be wrong."

"All right, Molie. I'll call the doctor and see what I can find out."

"Will you come to the hospital this morning?"

"If you need me. I do have a job . . ."

"Hurry, Randy, please hurry."

"I'll get somebody to take care of the girls, and then I'll come."

"But you'll call the doctor right now, won't you?"

"I said I would."

Molaine tried to take a deep breath and calm herself. It wasn't easy. She hadn't had any sleep, since the first feeding hour, and they hadn't brought her the baby. It began to be a long night, and the cries of the babies being wheeled to and from the nursery was part of the coldness that tightened over Molaine's heart.

"Good morning, Mrs. McGregary." The nurse came in with a breakfast tray, but Molaine didn't feel like eating.

"Good morning. I want to talk to the doctor. Nurse, can't you get my doctor?"

"The doctor will be making his rounds soon. He'll come in and talk to you then."

"But I need to see him before the next feeding time for the babies."

"I'll see what I can do. Now will you sit back and eat some breakfast? You'll need your strength to take care of your baby."

"Why? I mean, is there anything special about taking care of my baby?"

"There's something special about caring for every baby."

"I know that!" Molaine felt like she was listening to a pat lecture on the care and feeding of babies or why we have babies.

The stupid nurse, she was thinking. *Doesn't she know I already care? What is she trying to say? She's putting me off, just not telling me.* She pushed away the breakfast tray.

"Now, Mrs. McGreg. . ."

"Later," Molaine said irritably. "I can't eat now."

"I'll have to write that on your chart."

Molaine wanted to shout at her, "GO AHEAD!" but all she did was quietly nod and get out of bed.

The day wore on endlessly. Randy called. He couldn't find out anything from the doctor. Her doctor's secretary called to let her know he would be in to talk to her as soon as he had anything to report. And Molaine stewed. Back and forth around the room, down the hall, peaking in at the nursery, asking about little Randy.

"I would like to see the McGregary baby."

"I'm sorry, the McGregary baby isn't available."

The anxiety was driving her crazy. She walked. She read. She prayed and waited for Randy. When Randy finally came in during visiting hours, she almost collapsed in his arms, finally letting out her anxiety in a burst of tears.

"What did the doctor say, Randy?"

"He said he would check the baby and then talk to you. He's making some tests."

"Why won't they let me see him?"

"The doctor said he was in the incubator. Just until the tests were complete."

"Then there is something wrong?"

"Don't panic, Molie. We've got to have faith."

"But, Randy, this is our baby."

"There was another baby, Molie, one born to Mary in Bethlehem." Randy didn't know why he thought of Mary and the birth of Christ at that very moment; he hadn't been thinking that way, hadn't planned on saying anything like that at all. But as the words came out, they seemed to give him the power to give Molie courage. He didn't say anymore, but the words had their effect.

Molie drew a sudden quick breath and looked at Randy, the

sobs turned off, her shoulders relaxed, and Randy held her tightly in his arms.

"Molie, you have two wonderful girls at home and a small son in the nursery. We want him to have every chance, don't we?" Molaine nodded, her head tight against Randy's shoulder. "And knowing he is not only our son but also the son of our Father in Heaven, I think we can say a prayer for him, and for us, tonight and let his Father of Higher authority be in charge, don't you think?"

"Randy, he is so little."

"Our Father knows that. Come on, Honey, let's have our prayer and let me get back to the children. It won't be long until we know."

Holding each other, they prayed together, and Randy blessed Molaine and the baby and included the doctors and those who attended small Randy; then he kissed his wife.

"You get some sleep, Honey."

"Randy, don't you think it's a little ironic?"

"What?"

"This is the first time I have had such an easy birth that I didn't even lose my strength. I feel so strong, so ready to go home. I feel physically ready to go home with you right now, and yet this time I'm staying in the hospital for the baby, waiting for the baby."

"It won't be long. You look so beautiful, so thin already. . ."

She looked down at herself. "Except for all this milk that's coming in. Milk, milk everywhere, and they won't let me feed my baby a drop."

Randy kissed her again and then left her alone in the hospital as he had done the night before. This time there was a different feeling, a new faith. Randy wondered what it meant?

Molaine walked to the window to watch as Randy left the building and made his way to the car. Then, alone in her room, trying to shut out the happy baby talk around her, she picked up her white leather bound *Book of Mormon* that Randy had given her for their seminary graduation, which she always carried with her when she left home, got into bed, and began to read.

As she read the scriptures, she'd grown up on, many of them seemed to have new meaning, meaning to quench her immediate worries. Eagerly, she read from one to another, and as the quiet of the hospital began to radiate, and the patients went to bed, she read on and on into the night. The blessing Randy had given her filled her mind and tended her heart. As she read, she knew she was mentally praying. Then, as lights out on the floor reminded her, she shut the book and lay back against her pillow. A new glow was inside her.

"I have a son," she said aloud in the dark. "I know I have a son. I carried him for nine months inside me. I felt him move and was acquainted with his individual movements. He cried when he was delivered. I have a son. No matter what happens, whatever his mission, he is mine, as long as I live worthy to be his mother. And someday, even if now should not be the time, someday I will raise him to manhood. . ." She smiled in the dark with a new calmness. "Randy Norman McGregary . . . oh, Randy, we truly have a son."

She turned over, tucking the sheets around her body, looking out at the stars that were dimly seen through the top part of her window. "Thank you, Father," she breathed. "Thy will be done . . . whatever is Thy will . . ."

Breathing deeply, she thought of her two little daughters at home waiting for a new baby brother and prayed that it might be now, in this very life, that she would be given the opportunity to raise him. "I'll do my best, Father. I'll do my very best to raise him unto Thy will . . ."

Her eyes closed, and her breath came easy. It wouldn't be long before they had a report. . .

There was a click beside her door. The lights went on, and the doctor came in.

"I'm sorry I'm visiting so late, Mrs. McGregary. Is it all right if we talk a minute about your baby?"

"Doctor, is he all right?"

"I think so." The doctor came close to her bed. "I hope this light isn't too bright for your eyes."

"No, doctor. What about my baby?"

"I'm sorry I have taken so long, but I wanted to check everything I could. I did some tests this morning and had him out of the incubator this morning while I worked in the nursery, and he seems fine. I'd have been in before, but I had two scheduled operations. I just came from the other families."

"If he's all right, why won't the nurses bring him to me. I want to feed him."

"They will be bringing him around on the next feeding tour."

"Why didn't they bring him before?"

"The nurses were afraid for him. He's very white, which sometimes means poor circulation."

"But both of my girls were white, too. I don't have red babies."

"I thought perhaps you'd be able to tell me that. You see, your son was born with an odd heartbeat. It isn't anything consistent. I have seen beats like this before. Sometimes they disappear in a week or a few months. Sometimes they last all their lives, but I've never seen them do anything. They are just odd."

"Can I take him home?"

"I'm going to release both you and the baby in the morning."

"Oh, doctor, you just made me the happiest woman in the hospital."

"Well, I don't think there is any danger. I had him out of the incubator all morning while I worked in the nursery, and I didn't see any signs of blue or lack of breath in any way. For some strange reason his heart beats along just normally, and then, for no reason I can locate, it suddenly skips a beat. I want you to watch him very closely, sleep next to his bed for the next week or so, and learn to listen to his heartbeat. If you notice any change at all, call me, all right?"

"All right."

"I think all your son needs is a lot of good old mother's milk."

"Thank you, doctor." Molaine was radiant.

Promising to sign the check-out, the doctor turned off her light and left.

"Father, thank you. . ." breathed Molaine as she reached for the telephone beside her bed in the dim light and dialed her home. "Randy," she said softly when she heard his voice. "Randy, I can come home in the morning. Little Randy isn't out of danger. It might even be better for us to name him here in the hospital and give him a blessing here before we move him. But we can come home tomorrow. Will you come for us early?"

"I'll come for you early, and we'll give him a blessing. But we'll wait to name him in church the way we named both the girls. He's going to be just fine, Molie. I couldn't tell you that for sure this morning, but now I know."

"How do you know?"

"I just know. It's a feeling. This is a very special boy we have. He may grow up to be president of the country or of the Church. Trust me, Molie."

"Randy, you've never been this way about the other children. I'm usually the one with faith about the children."

"Usually, yes, Molie. But this time I have the strongest feeling. Don't you worry about little Randy."

Molaine felt better. She said good-night to Randy on the phone and had just settled herself for a good night's sleep when the light switch clicked on, and there was the nurse.

"Feeding time for your baby, Mrs. McGregary."

"Welcome news!" she said, sitting up.

Then, as the nurse put little Randy into her arms, she said, "You will be careful with him, won't you?"

"Of course, nurse. Why?"

"Well, he isn't normal, you know."

"Isn't he?" Molie smiled.

"Oh, no," said the nurse seriously. "There's something wrong with him. He's too white. Look . . ." the nurse walked back to the waiting baby beds and picked up a very red baby and held it up. "This is a normal baby, Mrs. McGregary. See? Red! Your baby is white."

"Oh," said Molaine, smiling broadly. "Well, it's all right, nurse. I'll take him anyway. You see, I have two more at home with just the same color of skin."

"**F**ive whole days . . ."

"And nights. . ."

"Randy, all ours to get away and be together, just the two of us? It must be heaven early, Christmas in July, gold in our own backyard. I can't believe it. If you pinch me and wake me, I'll . . . kill you."

"Kill me? Then who will take you on our vacation?"

"We've waited so long. Are you sure the boss won't change his mind the last minute and decide some big deal can't go through without you? That's happened twice before."

"He says this one is for real. So pack your bags, and let's get out of town before somebody finds out and keeps us home."

"I'm practically packed. Imagine, five days with just little old us to entertain and be with."

"You won't mind leaving the children, Molie?"

"Not with Mother. When you told me your days off had been approved, I thought, no, something will happen. We aren't that blessed, not along with all the other blessings we've had. Even when Mother said she'd come and stay with the children, even then, I thought it was too good to be real. But then there was still time for your boss to change his mind or me to break my leg or you to get another promotion that needs you right now . . . but . . ."

"But the time is now, and the plans are all set and approved of, and we are on our way."

"How long has it been, Randy? A real vacation?"

"Not since our honeymoon, not for a whole week anyway."

With exhilarating delight, the luggage came out. But there was more to getting ready for a five-day trip than just packing the clothes she and Randy would need. There was a day of baking, to leave home-made bread for the children, a day of getting the children's clothes ready, a day of washing and housecleaning, a day of finishing ward and stake work, turning over immediate responsibilities to someone else while they were away. There was a day of shopping to coordinate their clothes and all the talk that it took to orient the children to the understanding that they would be with Grandma a few days without parents. The day before it would be time to leave, Randy came home to find Molaine putting the last things in the bags, exhausted.

"You've worked so hard, you aren't going to have any fun. You'll be so tired that all you'll do is sleep."

"At least I'll be with you." She flopped into a chair beside the stack of clothes she had just finished folding. "I think I have everything ready for Mother. The kids are all well . . . I hope they stay that way while we're gone. If you'll give them an extra powerful blessing before we go . . ."

"How do you think little Randy will stand it without you? Pretty good timing . . . wean him and let your mother take over."

"I worry about him a little. I guess I've nursed him too long. I was going to have him drinking out of a glass by now. I'm sure Mother will think I'm odd. A year old and just finished nursing."

"He's been healthy, hasn't he?"

"Ever since his heart scare in the hospital, he hasn't even gotten the flu or colds with the girls. A week after I started nursing him that funny heartbeat was all gone. I've always thought it was the good mother's milk. The doctor thought that, too. But now he's off that and onto cow's milk. I hope that doesn't make any difference."

"Of course, it won't. He has a good start. Now let's get some sleep. I'll pick up your mother in the morning, and vacation, here we come."

Molaine couldn't believe how smoothly everything went toward the end. Their bags were in the car, the boat checked out for good running, the office had cooperated . . .

"Mother, I have frozen meals in the deep freeze. The numbers where we'll be are in the tablet beside the phone. Toni's friend's mother will pick her up for dancing. Vel has her piece memorized for Sunday School, just remind her to turn on the tape recorder and practice. Don't let Randy have sweets; he isn't used to them, and they might make him sick. He eats lots of fruits and vegetables. Home-made bread . . ."

"Molaine, go on your trip. Your children will be just fine."

"It's all too perfect. I can't believe it's happening to us. . ."

They were actually in the car leaving when the phone rang, and Randy was called back. When he joined Molaine again, she looked at him inquiringly.

"Was it the office?"

"How did you guess?"

"What did they want?"

"Not too bad. Jack has some plans that need to be checked out for that big job. You know the one I told him had to be completed. . . well, he's just finished them. The people are screaming, so he'll meet me down by the entrance of the lake, and I'll sign them for him. No big deal."

"Somehow a no-big-deal, for the office always ends up being a great big deal. What if he isn't there to meet us?"

"He will be. Don't worry."

"I don't like the way you say that, Randy."

As they drove away from the city, Molaine felt strange. Her mind began going over all the little things the children had said, the little things they did, and she was lonely before she was ten miles away. Randy, sensing her feelings, reached over to take her hand in his.

"We've earned some time to ourselves, you know, Molie."

"I know. I'm going to enjoy it, too."

"Do you think you can stand it with just me, or should we have invited a couple. Maria and Jack hinted they would like to come . . ."

"No, thanks, just enough of Jack to get the papers signed, that's all. It seems like we've been going so long and hard that we haven't even seen each other. I couldn't stand five days of prattle of how she decorated her kitchen and what new bedspread Maria is ordering for her freshly-decorated bedroom. I may be selfish, but this is my vacation, and I don't want to spend it with anyone but you . . . my Lord and Master."

"I'm glad you're like this, Molie. We haven't been too far apart through the years, have we?"

"The gap has been pretty big at times, Randy. Remember last year when you went on that convention without me?"

"You couldn't go. You had a nursing baby."

"He was your baby, too."

"But I wasn't nursing him."

"That's the point. I had to stay home, and you took off without me. I was really mad at you."

"You said it was all right."

"What else could I say? Inside I could have strangled you and felt good. I was so tired."

"The business has to go on."

"That's the dumbest thing I ever heard. The business doesn't depend on a convention."

"They help."

"Well, I forgive you now."

"I should be the one to forgive you. You went to see your mother for a whole week when I got back."

"I needed the rest."

"So now we're even, and this is for us . . . a second honeymoon."

But the second honeymoon took on a new look by the time they arrived at the lakesight where they were supposed to meet Jack and sign the papers. Jack was late, as usual, and when he did appear, it was not as a businessman but dressed in a sports outfit with Maria beside him.

"Sorry, old man," said Jack as he came across the lobby of the hotel where they were registered to stay for three days.

"We've been out on the golf course. This is a fantastic place, McGregary. How did you find it?"

"Part of my youth."

"What a place."

"Yeah, did you bring the papers for me to look over?"

"No hurry. Maria and I got the idea right after I talked to you on the phone. Since I didn't take all my vacation days, we thought we'd just stay on here for a while. We're killing two birds with one stone, if that's all right with you?"

"You? You're staying here at this hotel?" Randy could feel his chin drop in disbelief.

"Sure. You don't mind, do you? You said you were alone, so I didn't suppose you'd mind."

"Yeah, sure." Randy looked at Molaine, her eyes answering his, but she didn't say any words.

"We have the double room across the hall from you two. That way we can get up and golf together."

"This isn't really good golfing weather. We thought we'd water ski. . ."

"Maria likes that. Lucky we had to meet right now. I hate vacations alone. Maria and I get bored when we're alone. What about dinner tonight? My treat, old man . . ."

"We'll get our rooms and then talk about it, all.right, Jack?"

"This hotel is full. We were just lucky and got that last double. Did you have to have a double in your rooms?"

"I'll see what we get when I take my bags up. Come on, Molie."

"I knew it was too good to be true," whispered Molaine under her breath.

They went up to unpack and try to make the best of a bad situation. But the bad situations had only just begun. It was late afternoon when they were launching the boat on the lake that a plane came in, flying low and landed on the lake. It turned out to be Randy's Uncle Wilber, his wife Ann, and their two teenage children. As the plane taxied to the dock, Uncle Wilber called to Randy.

"I heard you were coming down here, Randy, but didn't

think there was a chance in the world I could find you."

"What are you doing here, Uncle Wilber?"

"Ann and I were bored and thought we'd take a chance on finding you. What about a quick water ski? We'll only be here today."

That was the beginning. Randy turned the boat around and waited while Uncle Wilber anchored the plane and came aboard. Then they spent the afternoon giving everybody rides on the water skiis, and by the time Randy could have taken a ride, the boat needed to be refueled, and after that it was too dark. A great afternoon, listening to stories of the family, stories of work. Molaine listened and wondered what the children were doing at home and felt like she was seeing everybody but Randy.

"It's just that we haven't even had a chance to talk for so long," complained Molaine when they were alone in their hotel room getting ready for dinner that they didn't want to go to. "This isn't my idea of a second honeymoon or even a vacation. It would have been better to bring the children along; at least we'd be giving them sharing time."

"I know, Molie. But what can we do? Let's just go out to dinner with them tonight. At least Jack is buying, and after filling the boat with gas both times, my ready cash is going fast."

"They didn't even offer to buy gas?"

"Jack said he'd be glad to give up a ride in his plane."

"Oh, good. Who wants a ride in his plane? I just want to be left alone."

"Hush, Honey. We can't treat people like that."

"Oh, can't we? I find out inside that I'm really not a very nice person when my plans are all switched around without my permission."

"It won't be long; they'll all leave by noon tomorrow."

"What if they don't?"

"They will. . ." But his words were interrupted by a knock at their door. Randy opened it to find Uncle Wilber.

"Randy, they haven't a room left in the hotel. They might have a possibility after dinner. We thought if you'd let us change in here with you, then we'd be able to find something after dinner. We won't need much, just a change of clothes and some suntan lotion. Ann is pretty burned from this afternoon."

"I'm pretty burned myself," said Molaine as she moved her luggage to one side while Wilber went to get the family.

"What can I do?" Randy shrugged his shoulders.

"Daddy, can I go home?" Molaine asked sarcastically. But she opened the door for Wilber and indicated the extra bed. "You can put your things there."

"Oh, how fortunate; you have a room with two beds."

"They were out of king size, so they gave us two regulars."

"Well, things aren't too bad then. If we can't get a room tonight, maybe a few hours sleep here . . . there is a partition to pull, isn't there?"

"I haven't really looked," said Randy, wondering if his uncle was only kidding.

"Well, it isn't like you were newlyweds. I wouldn't think of moving in with a couple of newlyweds, but . . . You know your father and I and our families shared a couple of rooms with fewer luxuries than we have here when we were in the service together. What a funny time that was . . . both of us stationed at Fort Williams . . . our wives came out to be with us, and there was only a one-room motel left in the whole town. We . . . "

But Molaine and Randy weren't hearing the rest of his story; they were looking at each other in disbelief, yet knowing it was getting ready to happen. They were thinking of sharing their extra bed. Randy and Molaine knew what they were thinking and yet didn't know how to stop them.

"We'll fly out of here in the morning, early. A few hours' sleep, and we'll leave you to yourselves."

For real! When the chatter of dinner was over and they'd eaten too much too fast and talked too much too long, the six of them retired into two hotel rooms with double beds and a pull door between the beds. Molaine was shivering as she climbed into bed, turned her face to the wall and quietly sobbed.

"What a mess." She sobbed brokenly as Randy put his arm around her. "Don't touch me. This is the worst vacation I've ever had in my life."

"Don't get mad at me; it isn't my fault."

"I'm not mad at you," she said in a loud whisper and would have shouted if they had been alone.

"It's my fault. I should have stayed home with my children."

"How can you say that? You had me before you had the children. Don't I fit into your life anywhere, Molie?"

"You and all your relatives and your office personnel."

"But it isn't my fault," Randy persisted.

"I know that, Randy. I wish it was, then I could cuss you for it and feel better. Oh, how can people be like this?"

"Like Uncle Wilber says, a few hours' sleep and they will be on their way. And it isn't like we were on our honeymoon." Randy smiled a sick little smile, and Molaine threw her pillow at him.

But in the morning Molaine felt uptight and unrested. She got up early to get her shower and leave the hotel room so Aunt Ann could get ready.

"We left our children home," she said as she and Randy went to get some juice to take in the boat cooler, but instead we have your teenage cousins with us."

"It's all over now. They'll be leaving this morning. We still have one more night."

But it wasn't over. They had trouble with the fan belt on the plane, and they spent the whole morning running around to get it fixed. When Uncle Wilber, his wife, and children were finally on their way home, there was only time for a quick boat ride. Jack was checked out on the controls, so Randy could ski, then they started home but got lost on the lake in one of the coves. It was too dark to see their way out, so the four of them stayed all night on the boat, the waves splashing the sides of the boat, and the sky swinging back and forth above them.

By the time they checked out of their hotel room and had everything loaded to start home the next day, Molaine wasn't even speaking to Randy. They drove in silence. Molaine was even too angry to cry anymore.

"Won't this car go any faster?"

"Can't stand to spend another hour with me, huh?"

"I just want to get home, Randy. I mean this whole trip has been one disaster after another. We've spent our vacation money and time, and we haven't done anything except entertain everybody else. I should have stayed home with the children. It just shows how dumb I am to ever try and leave."

"We have to try. It wasn't our fault."

"How does that help? Just get me home. When I think of all I have left for my mother, how I've deserted the children to be with Uncle Wilber and that boring Maria and Jack. . . I have never had such foolish conversations. Do you know that Maria took thirty minutes to tell me exactly how she prepares a Sunday roast? And how to cook corn. Do you know there are at least three or four ways to cook corn. How it tastes depends on the amount of spice, and you never add the spice until it's time to eat it or . . . it was all so dumb."

"Jack had a good time showing me up in golf."

"And so he should when he hasn't anything to do but play golf. He hasn't any children or . . . some people live such shallow lives. One day with my children is more rewarding than decorating her whole house."

"But it won't help to be upset, will it?"

"No, it won't help to be upset."

They drove along in silence again. Then suddenly Randy began to laugh.

"Something funny?"

"Yes, it is. I think of Uncle Wilber snoring on the other side of the petition. Do you know he snored half the night?"

"Oh, I thought that was just a slight earthquake."

"No, the earthquake was when Ann took that last fall on the water skiis."

"And when the plane wouldn't start?" Randy shrugged and looked at Molaine. He reached for her hand, and they started laughing, laughing and relating the stupid things they had gotten into. They laughed and laughed. To finish off, there was a sudden noise, and the air went out of one of the front tires.

"That makes it complete. Now we'll change to our only spare tire and get to the nearest service station."

Together they got out and unloaded the trunk to get the spare tire. They put it on and started down the road. They hadn't gone very far when another tire went flat.

"Well, that's it. I haven't anymore spares. We'll have to get a ride to the nearest service station and fix one."

"This is scarry, Randy. What if the wrong person stops?"

But the wrong person didn't stop. A nice farmer gave them a ride to a service station, and they got a wrecker to haul them in. By the time the car was ready for the trip, it was dark.

"We can't make it home in time for work tomorrow, Randy."

"We might just be forced to stay." Randy looked around. They were at the top of a canyon. It was a pretty stop with a nice motel across the road and the sun just setting in a beautiful red glow. "There's a trail leading to the ridge. We could hike up there in the morning and overlook the whole valley."

"This is almost like our honeymoon motel, remember?"

"I remember. The motel has a swimming pool."

"Well, what are we waiting for?"

"We had car trouble, right?"

"Right."

Smiling like a couple of friends out on an adventure, Randy turned to talk to the service station attendant.

"Take your time, Mister. Fix the car up good. We're going to be staying overnight."

Taking out an overnight bag, they made their way across the street.

"I guess you can let the boss know you had some car trouble."

"I guess I can. Remind me to do that in the morning."

With a broad smile, Molaine nodded. "I'll remember to remind you." Then with her hand in his, they ran across the road to register for a motel for the night, feeling happy, a little guilty, and like a couple of kids in love.

9

When little Jesica was born, Randy and Molaine were ready for a new baby. Jesica weighed seven and a half pounds, was bright-eyed, and a darling baby from the very beginning. It was another new community; they loved the semi-city location, had immediately become involved in school, civic and church affairs, and they took time to enjoy the new baby.

"I appreciate the children even more as I get older," announced Randy as he sat beside the fire, burping Jesica.

"And you have your built-in baby sitters." Toni reached for Jesica.

"I thought you didn't want a new baby, Toni," Randy teased.

"I didn't want to share things with her, but now that she's here it's all right with me."

"A sheer bundle of joy," Molaine announced, and so she was with everyone making a fuss over Jesica. But there were still problems in the family.

Vel was old enough to start school when Jesica was born. Vel had followed Toni around from the beginning, doing all the things her older sister did. She couldn't wait to go to school.

"Vel has never had any friends her own age, Randy." Molaine was putting the finishing stitches on a little green school dress for Vel to wear her first day. She's been the only girl her age in this whole area. She's always had to play with friends older or younger."

"That won't hurt her. Mother said that we didn't need friends; we had each other. Brothers and sisters play together, was what Mother always said."

"She does that, but it seems like it's hard for her to stay with the older ones. When school starts, I think she'll find some friends."

So on the first day of school, as Molaine stood in line with Velvet in her new green dress that made her skin look so beautiful, two mothers were standing in line with their little girls who were obviously close friends. One mother said to Molaine, "Your daughter's hair is so beautiful, and she looks so lovely in that green dress."

Molaine smiled and squeezed Vel's hand, but she noticed that one little girl of the two mothers that had spoken, said to the other, "I think she's ugly, don't you?"

"I think she's really ugly. We won't play with her."

So Vel hadn't gotten off to a very good start with the new group, and the first day she was left to ride the bus home, she came home crying because the two little girls had taken turns spanking her on the way home.

"It's a problem, Randy. I have to go with her to the bus every day and meet her when she gets off. Those little girls were just jealous because of what their mothers said, but I can't make Vel see that. She just knows that they don't want to play with her, and that hurts."

Vel had only been in school about two weeks when she started complaining about her leg hurting. At first, Molaine didn't think much of it, but every day she complained.

"I'm worried about her, Randy. I think I'll have the doctor check her."

But the doctor didn't find anything.

"These little ones often have growing pains. We'll give her some warmth treatments. It might be some aches or maybe an attention getter."

"Don't you think we should x-ray the leg, Doctor?"

"I don't think so. We'll just give her some vitamin shots and watch her."

That evening Velvet had a temperature and was too sick to get out of bed the next morning. Her temperature went down in the morning and up in the evening, and she couldn't eat anything and keep it down. Randy gave her a blessing, and Molaine fasted and prayed. It was frightening to see her little thin body. Then the morning after her blessing her temperature was down, and she was splashed from head to foot with red spots.

"Vel, you have the measles, the red measles. You had us fooled, and now that you've broken out, you should be much better."

But breaking out in measles was only the beginning of her problems. When she was well from the measles, she still cried with pain in her leg. All night long Molaine prayed, and she seemed to think, *x-ray that leg, x-ray that leg.*

In the morning she called the doctor and made an appointment, but she could tell he thought she was just being neurotic. "I think she needs some extra attention." Molaine was angry.

She spoke to Randy at breakfast. "She has never been that kind of child, to put on a show for attention. There's something wrong; I know it."

Just to make sure, Molaine watched when Velvet went to play with Toni and her friends. It was her first day out after the measles, and as Molaine watched, when the kids ran, Velvet would run after them and drag her leg.

"She wouldn't do that, Randy," she said that evening. "She didn't know I was watching. She was just trying to stay up with Toni. You know what a fighter she is. She would have stayed up with them if she could. There has to be something very serious. I'm taking her back to the doctor, and this time I want that leg x-rayed."

This time the doctor listened, and they x-rayed Velvet's leg. Molaine felt better after the x-rays and went home to wait for the results. Then they found it. The doctor called her after consulting an x-ray specialist.

"She has a softening of the hip bone, Mrs. McGregary. It's what we call Perthe's Disease."

"What causes it, Doctor?"

"We don't know."

"But I've fed her the same things I've fed the other children. What could have caused this? What do I do for it?"

"The only treatment we have used so far is to take the weight off the leg. I'm calling in a bone specialist."

Then the fear began to clutch at Molaine's throat. She worried during the day and had dreams by night, and in all the dreams she was always looking for Velvet and always before she found her something had happened. There was something wrong.

There were appointments with the specialist and doctor, and they talked about treatment. Again, Molaine learned to live by fasting and prayer, clinging to faith like one going down for the last time in a pool of dark water. Fighting to hold on to her faith, sobbing out her hurt in prayer, crying out for guidance and understanding. And all the while, little Velvet seemed to get weaker, and her little bones showed through her clothing. They prayed as a family and individually, and Molaine found herself pleading for answers, for understanding, praying those who made the decisions would be guided.

"She's going to get well, Randy. I know she's going to get well."

"What are they going to do for her? What have the doctors decided?"

"They all agree that the only treatment is to take her weight off her hip, hoping the body will heal the bone. Taking the weight off should help the bone in the socket to stay round and not go flat."

"That's all they have?"

"That's all they have. But I'm not going to leave it there. I'm going to study everything I can get my hands on and search for answers and never give up. I'll never give up. If Father can save her, He can also make her well."

"If it is His will."

"I'm not going against His will, Randy. I want to be obedient, I want to be a good mother and lead the children in righteousness, but we are also supposed to do all we can and to have faith. I have that faith. Unless there is a good reason for Vel to be other than whole, she will get well."

There were several ways they could take the weight off Velvet's hip. The one they decided on was a little harness with a buckle to hold the leg up while she walked on crutches. While waiting for Vel's fitting, Molaine conquered herself and her hurts privately. She was ready to give courage and help, to smile and look at everything in a positive way, determined that Velvet would be positive, too.

Then, at last the day Velvet was to be fitted with a harness and crutches finally came. Molaine put her in the car and went to the clinic.

At first the nurse took her measurements and sewed a little harness that went on like a jacket made of straps with a little pad that went around her ankle. There were buckles on the strap around her ankle and matching ones on the harness, so that when her leg was tied up, it looked like she had one leg off.

Then she was measured for crutches that fit just right under her little arms. After all the measuring, she stood there looking down at herself. Her leg tied up, the harness around her waist and over her shoulders.

"Aren't they the cutest little crutches you've ever seen?" Molaine forced herself to be excited. Velvet looked down at herself, and a weak smile crossed her lips. She nodded. Then she looked down at herself once more and asked quietly, "Mother, would you mind carrying me to the car?"

Unable to talk, Molaine tucked her handbag under Velvet's arm, picked her up, crutches and all, and walked out to the car waiting beside the curb.

Velvet had been down with the measles and Perthe's Disease for almost three weeks. She had missed a lot of school. Arriving home, Molaine settled her in the front room on the couch, her crutches beside her, her dolls and drawing papers on the little table in front of her—the spot where she had spent most of every day since her leg had started to hurt.

"Now, if you want to walk, the crutches are right here, Vel."

"Thanks, but I won't need to walk."

"Just in case you want to. You'll need to use your crutches to walk."

"I can hop, can't I?"

"Yes, you can hop, but that will make you tired very quickly. It isn't hard to walk on crutches; you'll see."

Molaine went into the kitchen, leaving Velvet to ponder, to draw, play with dolls, or to try walking on her crutches. With her heart in her mouth and a prayer on her lips, Molaine forced herself to hum a tune while she worked over the kitchen sink. Then she heard it, a clonk, clonk, clonk . . . and she knew Velvet was trying her crutches. She looked up with a smile as Velvet came through the hall door.

"You've learned how to use them already."

"I can walk on them, but I don't have to go to school on them, do I?"

"No, you don't have to go to school on them unless you want to go to school." And Molaine wondered what she would do if Velvet didn't want to go to school. The doctors hadn't given any encouragement as to how long until the hip joint healed. That could be a long time, and Molaine knew that Velvet had to go to school. Refusing to cry, smiling instead, she began to pray again.

Around and around the house, through the hall, into the bedrooms, back into the front room, she wouldn't stop. It was as if the three weeks of illness had built up inside her, and she couldn't get enough of moving. Then into the kitchen again, and she made her way past Molaine to the kitchen door that lead to outside and the backyard. She stood beside the door.

"Will you open the door for me, Mother?"

Everything inside Molaine wanted to shout and say, "No, that's enough for one day. You need rest, you need to get well, you've done too much . . . ." But all she did was move to the door, open it, and hold the screen.

"Do you want me to help you?"

"Just hold the door. I can do it."

"Shall I go with you?"

"No. I want to go alone."

Molaine moved aside, holding the door open with her hand as Vel stepped past her, down the four little steps leading to the backyard, and then Molaine listened as the crutches made their light clonks along the sidewalk . . . then she heard it, a crash!!! Molaine opened the door and almost flew to her daughter.

She was down, the little crutches hitting the cement hard, and the little knee, doubled out in front, was forced to take the blow of the fall. Molaine picked her up. She wasn't crying. Then she looked down at her knee, where it hit, and there was a small red spot of blood on the center of her knee. When Velvet saw the blood, she started to cry. She put her arms around Molaine's neck and sobbed. And Molaine knew she wasn't sobbing just because her knee hurt but sobbing out the fears, the hours of illness, the fears and the anxieties of the long weeks of illness. She was crying for all the things she couldn't do now and the hurts of the harness and the crutches.

Molaine held her for a long time, and Velvet didn't see the tears that slipped down her mother's face. All she knew was the tenderness of her arms, the softness of her words in her ears, and the soft singing voice that hummed in her ear long after she had carried her to the bedroom, until she finally fell asleep. And then she prayed. Long into the night Molaine prayed. And then there was little Jesica that awakened in the night to be nursed, whose good health and shining eyes gave Molaine courage that her Father in Heaven was close and somehow would show her the way.

Quite miraculously the next morning Velvet was up and dressed before breakfast was ready.

"I'm going to school today," she announced as if she had never considered anything else.

"And you look so beautiful, too. We'll make it a special day. I'll take you to school in the car; you won't need to ride the bus today."

"Super!" Velvet reached for her lunch sack. "I can carry that with my crutches; it will fit under my hand."

From the minute Molaine and Velvet entered the school building, Velvet was number one popular girl. The children all came to greet her. Those who had been unkind to her before now were most willing to be the first to greet her. The class made get-well cards for her, and each one who dared ask was begging for a turn to try her crutches. It was the opening of a new era for Velvet. She was suddenly queen of her class.

With a grateful heart, Molaine returned home to take care of Jesica and pray her thanksgiving.

With Velvet happy at school, the children came by early in the morning with their wagon to pull her to the bus stop. And they bargained to take turns on her crutches like Tom Sawyer white washing the fence. But the worry of the cause and the cure were still on Molaine's mind night and day, day and night. Thinking about Vel's little bones and the reasons for the experience was a constant strain on Molaine. Randy was worried about Molaine and talked to her about it.

"You know, this isn't effecting Velvet at all. She handles crutches, friends, and all very well. You're the one making yourself ill, Molie."

"I know, Randy, but we've got to find a cure. I'm studying foods. Foods have to make some difference. If they could do anything to help her heal . . . but the medical doctors haven't any more answers. Just take her weight off the hip, that's all . . . and x-ray her."

"Then you're doing all you can."

"No. I'll do more. She's got to get well."

"You need to get it off your mind sometimes, Molie. Everyday I come home, I can tell how Vel is just by looking at your face."

"Do I show that much?"

"You show every feeling."

"If you can see it, then she can, too. I've got to change my attitude and find some answers for my worries."

So back to prayer, and this time Molie called for an appointment with the new Bishop of her new ward. She went to meet him.

"Bishop, I need a job in the ward. I can't handle a big job because I need to be available for Vel and the baby, but a small job. I need to serve somewhere to keep me sane."

So Molaine became assistant Beehive teacher, and within two weeks she was the only Beehive teacher. On her first night alone with the class, when they went into their individual rooms, some of her Beehive girls came running to her.

"Myra is leaving; she's going out on a date with a married man."

"She's what?"

"She's meeting him out front. That's what she says."

Molaine hurried to the front door where she found Myra putting on her coat.

"Aren't you coming to class, Myra?"

"No, I'm going on a date; my boyfriend is waiting." Molaine looked through the open door to the face of a man, waiting beside an old car. He was old enough to be Myra's father if not grandfather.

"Not with him? You aren't going out with him?"

"Sure I am." She pushed Molaine's hand off her arm.

"But why? Why not come to class? You don't want to go with someone like that."

"Yes, I do," she almost shouted. "Everything that can happen to me has already happened, and I don't care anymore." Jerking away, she ran through the open door into the waiting car where the older man didn't even have the courtesy to come for her or let her in the car. . . .

As Molaine made her report to the Bishop and went to join her class to teach a lesson, she was thinking, *Everything that can happen to me has already happened. I don't care anymore . . . there are worse things. There are worse things that can happen to my children than Perthe's Disease.*

10

Randy reached for Molaine's hand as she passed him where he sat by the fire in the front room.

"Come and sit beside me."

"The children aren't settled yet."

"They'll settle. I have a meeting in a few minutes, and I haven't seen you all day."

"All day? I haven't seen you to talk to for . . . well, let's see . . . . we do have time for a quick kiss goodbye after our morning prayer." Randy pulled his wife down beside him into the big chair.

"We can still fit into this chair. I guess we aren't ready for a divorce yet."

"Nope. This is the chair. You said if ever I got too big to fit into it . . ."

"Or if I do . . ."

"No chance of that; you'll look young even when you are ninety."

"Are you convinced of that?"

"More than convinced. I've imprinted you on my mind."

"Is it so important, Randy, how I look?"

"Of course. You'll always be young and beautiful like you are now."

"I'm afraid you will have a shock coming in about twenty

years."

"No, I won't. I've decided that how we look to each other is according to how we feel. If we're always in love, you'll always be young and beautiful."

"Randy, I hope you are good at imagining."

"I'm the best. I've been taught by an expert."

"Who?"

"You. You have such an imagination, Molie."

"How can you say that, Randy? I'm a completely logical person. Just what do I imagine that isn't true?"

"You imagine we're rich. You talk like we are wealthy."

"We are. I don't want for anything, Randy. I have a dishwasher, the best vacuum cleaner on the market, the children have plenty to eat, and we have an extra car, and there isn't anything we can't have if we are willing to give up something else to get it. We're rich."

"I know. You're a blessing to a husband, and you haven't had a new dress in a long time."

"I can make one if I want one."

"Have you ever gone downtown and just bought a dress?"

"Last year on my birthday you took me, remember? Besides, I prefer making my own clothes because I can make them fit better that way. What's the matter with you tonight, Randy? You aren't usually like this, so sentimental and . . . what's happened?"

"I don't know. I guess I was just thinking. One of the men at work, you know, John . . . I told you his work hadn't been up to what he usually does for quite a while?"

"Yes."

"Well, I found out why. He's been having trouble with his wife for quite a while now, and finally she just left him. She ran off with another guy and just left him."

"How sad."

"Yes, it is sad. He was a good producer. But I think it was his fault as much as hers."

"Why?"

"He's kind of a show off with the women. He likes to take his secretary to lunch and always tells them jokes, not always clean jokes. I could see he was headed for trouble one way or another last year. We talked about it a little, and he thought I was pretty stuffy. Well, now his wife has decided to play his own game, I guess. Anyway, he looks like something the dogs had been chewing on. He has three kids. They are the ones that will really suffer."

"Yes. The kids always suffer."

"Molie, while we're being serious, I need to thank you."

"For what?"

"Remember when I was first made an executive with a secretary of my own, and you made me promise I would never take my secretary to lunch without at least two other people with us?"

Molaine smiled and straightened. Randy pulled her closer to him. "Well, I admit I thought you were being a little silly at the time. I even thought you were just being prematurely jealous; I was even a little digusted with you, but you made me promise before I left for that convention, remember?"

"I remember."

"Well, you were right. I've been glad I made that promise more than once. I work with some pretty girls in our main office now. More than one. They are very good to me, and it would be easy to be close to them, not deliberately setting out for an affair, but I can see how it could happen very innocently. I spend more time at the office sometimes than I do at home. That's what happened to John. He's a good guy. He was just a little too friendly, just a good guy having a little fun, and he liked taking his secretary to lunch. I guess it made him feel young. Anyway, his wife found out, and he's been living in a living hell ever since. Finally, they just couldn't communicate anymore, and she met this guy and just left him. I've known there was something wrong for a long time."

"We do get ourselves into such a mess, don't we?"

"Yeah. I was just being grateful, thinking how little I do for you really and how loyal you are."

"Randy, you don't do just a little; you give us everything you've got."

"I know, but sometimes it's a world of let's-pretend-it's-perfect, for you, isn't it?"

"I resent that, Randy McGregary." Molaine sat up quickly, pointing her finger into his chest. She tapped him as she spoke. "I am a very practical person. I know I could go buy a dress if I wanted one. Is that what's bugging you? I know I could, but I don't want to. There are other things more important to me. I am so grateful for little Velvet. She's such a blessing to us, Randy. She has an effect on all the children; they are nicer to each other because they are nicer to her. She seems to radiate that special spirit of goodness wherever she is."

"How long has it been now?"

"She's been on crutches almost two years now. She's getting better; I know she is."

"What did her x-rays show?"

"The same. They can't see any change. But there's a change in Velvet. Her color is better, she's brighter, her eyes are brighter."

"Could you be just a mother?"

"I could be. But I know my daughter. She's getting better."

"I'm proud of you, Molie. You've handled the situation very well. If faith will get her well, she'll be better."

"It's more than faith. It's an inner feeling and a lot of work. I've studied everything I can get my hands on. She eats better. The whole family eats better. It's been the greatest experience of my life."

"You are saying you crave problems?"

"No. I don't want anymore. But all problems are growing experiences. I know that, and I'm grateful for what I've learned. But I'm not the kind to ask for more just so I can learn."

"You've been very practical about Velvet. I don't think her personality has suffered at all."

"She attributes her happiness and popularity to her crutches. She's really amazing. I was at school yesterday for their Christmas program. I couldn't believe Jesica. I was so proud, I was bursting. If I hadn't been that proud, I'd have been crying the whole time. Randy, when Velvet did the folk dances, she danced on her crutches back and forth, then she'd flop her crutch down, and she would hop around her partner. Then she'd pick up the crutch and dance again. That was quite an experience."

"How do the other children react to that?"

"They treat her like she's queen of the ball. And I can't tell you how many mothers came up to me to tell me how much Velvet had done for their children. I've had calls from mothers I haven't even heard of. One mother said her little son had his father cut him a strong willow so he could play crutches. He puts that willow under his arm and hops around like Velvet does. Which reminds me, Velvet and Toni should be getting home any minute now."

"Where are they?"

"Tending the Beckstead's children. There isn't any school tomorrow, and Velvet wanted to go with Toni. I told them not past ten. Just about that."

"Velvet's illness hasn't hurt her personality at all. You're the one who suffers. You still worry, don't you?"

"Not really. I've learned so much. I wouldn't want to go through it again, but I could never have learned what I've learned any other way."

They were sitting in the dark, with only the firelight and the kitchen lights cutting the darkness. An automobile came in the driveway, and the lights of the car shone through the window.

"Randy, they'll think we're sitting here making out."

"Well, aren't we? Come here, I'm going to give them a thrill and kiss you just as they come in."

"Randy, you act like a high school boy."

"High school was never like this. . ." She laughed as he kissed her, and the girls came in to tease them just as Randy knew they would.

"Come in, Velvet; Mom and Dad are sitting here making out. I caught them kissing."

"Who has a better right? I married your mother, and her kisses cost me plenty."

"Randy. . ." Molaine got up out of the chair where they sat together. "Did you girls do a good job? I was just beginning to worry."

"We did all right. Only Velvet got mad at Pete."

"What's the matter with Pete, Vel?"

"Mother, he said I was a cripple. I'm not a cripple, am I?"

"People are thoughtless in the things they say, Vel," Randy started to say. Molaine picked up the cue.

"Not really, Randy. They just don't understand."

"Why did Pete say I'm a cripple?"

"Maybe because you are. Do you know what it means to be a cripple, Vel? We're all cripples in one way or another."

"A cripple can't walk, Mother. I can walk."

"Sometimes a cripple can walk but has a broken arm. Cripple means some part of us doesn't work very well. That's all."

"Like my dog when he got a thorn in his paw and had to walk on three legs instead of four?"

"Yes, Vel, just like that."

"But my dog got better, and then he could walk on all his legs again."

"When he got better, he wasn't a cripple anymore. When you get better, you won't be a cripple anymore."

"When will I get better, Mother?"

"We don't know just when; we only know that you will get better, all right?"

"All right," Vel yawned. "I'm sleepy. Can I go right to bed?"

"When your teeth are brushed. You wouldn't want to cripple your teeth by putting holes in them. And be quiet in front of Jesica's room; she had a little problem getting to sleep tonight. No babysitters to spoil her."

The children went off to their rooms, and Randy sat looking into the fire again. "No matter how long it takes for Vel to walk again, she'll be all right because she has you."

"And the rest of the family, we've learned to live with a disability. We've learned a lot. Other people just don't understand. You know how it is. When she wears a dress, she looks like she has one leg off. Well, the other day in the store a lady by the checkstand said, right out loud, 'Oh, your poor little girl.' Vel looked up at me, and I looked at her; then I patted her on the head in an exaggerated movement and said, 'Oh, Vel, you poor little girl.' We both laughed all the way to the car. When you get used to living with a problem, it isn't a problem anymore."

"Yeah, unless the problem tears our world apart. I don't know what's going to happen with John. He really loves his family. He was just foolish, and now it's too late for him to change."

"Maybe he'll learn."

"For another family maybe; it's too late for this one. It makes me hurt all over, Molie, just to look at how he hurts."

"It's the little things that bless and change life, caring about little things, being honest in little things. You're a good husband, Randy."

"I might not have been, but problems keep me humble. I'm always struggling for more money."

"I hope we don't ever have too much . . . not until the children are on their own. Then maybe money won't hurt us."

"Speaking of problems, I have the chance for another promotion. Want to sell the house and move?"

"Oh, Randy, no. The children are just established."

"We can turn it down."

"But you want to take it, don't you?"

"It will mean a better job, more opportunities, and a good place to live in the West, close to the headquarters of the Church."

"We'll take it."

"How do you think the children will react?"

"The way we react. No big deal . . . a real opportunity. They will think so, too."

"It's true. They do react the way we do. Some of the guys in the company have a hard time getting their families to cooperate, but I think it's their own reaction, not their family's. Or maybe they just don't communicate."

"Every move has been a time of growth. But I would like to get a permanent home by the time they reach high school . . . for me, not them."

Randy laughed and pulled her down beside him again. "After this move, the boss says I can write my own ticket and stay there."

"Good. Will this be our dream house we build by ourselves?"

"Could be."

11

They built their first home the following summer. All the children helped. They contracted some of it out and did the painting and landscaping themselves. They were busy and happy, and problems seemed at a minimum. Randy's job was doing well, and it seemed like they had more money than ever before. That was the year Molaine got her sailboat for Christmas. She had always talked about having a sailboat but didn't really think she'd ever get one. But there it was, under the Christmas tree. It was only a small 12-foot dingey, but it filled the whole front room. Molaine was shocked with surprise.

The family spent home evenings that winter learning to tie knots and learning the language of boats. The Fore and Aft rig, the keel, rudder, sheet, and tiller. Then summer came, and the family put all their money together and bought a small building lot on the lake which was only a few hours' drive away. From then on, they didn't ever seem to have any extra money, but they always had a place to spend warm summer days whenever they could get away from work.

At first they put up tents on their lot, and then they built a small pumphouse where they slept at night and cooked over a campfire. Then gradually they put together a cabin with bedrooms. Those were the fun times, building a cabin of practically nothing but work and scraps. In the winter, they saved things for the cabin in the summer. Nails, old furniture, extra blankets. It was all for the lake. They spent the Christmas following the sailboat to sew sleeping bags, made of quilting blocks of old clothes. It was wonderful, a place to look forward to being together, and projects to hold them together while they dreamed. Thinking of the lake, the sun and sand became a refuge to look forward to, putting all the hurts and problems and Velvet's crutches into the background. They were always looking forward to summer and playtime at the lake. It was a place Molaine could give them the rules and not have to nag them, a time of freedom and working together.

Toni was in high school the summer they learned to sail. They had each had a chance to go out for a turn at sailing and a few instructions. It wasn't a dangerous boat. Every part would float. Randy bought a center hold for the sailrope for Molaine's birthday. It was to save her hands when the wind was right.

One day Toni took a boyfriend, Bill, out for a sail. It was a pretty day, not much wind. Randy and Randy Norman had gone fishing. Molaine was alone at the cabin. She watched Toni and Bill as they made their way out onto the lake.

"I think they are out too far, Velvet. You sit here and watch that boat. I'm not sure Toni knows a lot about sailing."

"Randy Norman said when the boat goes over he just stands on the side and flops it back up."

"Yes, but I wonder if Toni knows how to do that?"

"It won't sink, will it, Mother?"

"No, she's a sturdy little dingey, but I'm not ready to have her too far from shore."

As they watched, the sail went down. They went on watching, but the sail didn't come back up.

"I think they are in trouble. I'd better get the neighbors to take me out their in their motor boat. You go on watching and tell me what's happening. I'll get you the glasses so you can keep the spot. The wind's coming up. I'm worried."

The neighbors along the lake were all used to troubles in the waters and came to help each other. This time it was quite a hassle. The waves were coming up, as they often did in a few minutes after a calm. The motor boat would wash in when they took the anchor rope off. So, with enough people along the shore to hold it out until the motor was started, they took off toward the spot where Molaine had last seen the white sail go down.

"I think it went over about here, but why can't we see anything?" Molaine was more worried than she wanted to admit. "It's getting cold, too. I'll bet the kids are freezing in their wet suits."

"If the waves calm down," said the helpful neighbor, "we can probably spot them pretty easy."

"There's a boat coming this way. I wonder if they've seen them?"

It was a boat all right, and sitting on the front was Toni waving her arms. The boat slowed when it came in sight, and the neighbor cut his motor. The waves were high enough that Toni couldn't get off one boat on to the other, so she had to plunge in and swim for the ladder.

"We turned over and can't get the boat upright again. I hitched a ride with this boat to come and get some help."

"I knew you were in trouble, but with the waves we couldn't find you."

"Right ahead, you'll see."

Swinging the motorboat around, they made their way in the direction that Toni had come. And there she was. The family's favorite sailboat, upside down, the sail pointing straight down into the water, and Bill sitting on top.

"I don't think you've quite gotten the idea about sailing. . ." Molaine couldn't help laughing. "I think the sail goes the other way."

"Oh, I thought something was wrong," said Bill, embarrassed that a small sailboat could make him feel so foolish.

"The sail should be lying flat on the water. You must have had the centerpiece latched down."

"We did, Mom. It was holding good." Toni jumped in the water to swim to the sailboat.

"That's the idea, when you are in trouble, you let the center rope hang free. We'll have to dive under and pull it loose, or the sail won't come up."

It was hard work, but with the help of the neighbors, bailing water, and taking the sail apart under water, the boat was soon upright enough to be towed in. It was one of the crazy times they laughed about the rest of the day when the work was done.

The problems that taught the family to love the lake were problems never the less. Getting stuck in the sand was a constant dig-out. They built docks and anchored them off shore in the lake, and a storm would pull them loose and drag them to the other side of the lake. They were always looking for lost equipment in the water. But the lakeshore people were cooperative, all having the same kind of problems.

There was the time the little fishing boat was anchored on the bouy.

"It will be all right there," said Randy as he left to go with some of the men for a day in the stream. "It has plenty of slack, just let it stay there tied up."

Molaine followed his direction, but when night came, Randy still wasn't back. It wasn't uncommon for the men to stay overnight in the hills if they found some good fishing. So Molaine didn't worry too much. But in the night a storm came up, a terrible storm, and Molaine worried about the fishing boat. She got up in the night to shine the flashlight on the water. It was raining, and the wind was blowing the rain until it was hard to see at all. But the boat wasn't there. Molaine went back in the cabin to wake Randy Norman.

"The little boat is gone. We've got to find it, or the motor will be ruined."

"We can't do anything until morning, Mom."

"We can find out where it is and maybe save it."

Together they got dressed, putting plastic bags over their heads, with a hole cut for the face, and went out into the rain with a flashlight. Walking along the shore, they tried to see through the dark.

"The wind is blowing this way; it would have had to wash down onto the shore somewhere close to here."

"But how far? Mom, this is crazy."

"I know. We should have gotten someone to pull it out of the water. Your father's car has the boat hitch, and he said to leave it, but we could have found someone to get it out. I'm afraid the motor will be wet."

"Well, we'll never find it tonight. I'm soaked, Mom. We'd better go back and wait for daylight."

And then they heard a scraping sound, sounding like metal on metal. They had come to a fence on the beach, and they started up by the fence. There it was. The little boat washing against the fence, crashing against the steel posts with every wave. It was completely beached.

"Come on, Mom. It's here."

They examined the boat with their flashlight. It was full of water, but the motor was still latched up and high enough that it only got the splash of the waves. Together they unplugged the motor, a small ten-horse power, took it off the boat, and struggled home with it. The boat had to stay against the fence until morning.

But there were never enough troubles on the lake to make the family want to stay away. There were some heartaches, though, like the year the little girl was washed overboard in a storm and was lost. They never did find her body. There were rules people were supposed to follow, rules about life jackets, and whenever anyone violated them, there were tragedies. But for the family, the lake was a time to laugh and play, and Mom's sailboat was an object for learning lessons.

"Randy, you've been the one to teach us how to laugh," Molaine said with her head on his shoulder, sleepy from too many nights up, as they drove home through the night. They'd stayed too long at the lake and needed to make it home in time for Sunday meetings the next morning.

"The lake has been a good investment. I don't suppose we'll ever have a glamorous cabin, a summer home like most people, but our cabin keeps us busy. When you first bought the land on the lake and that sailboat, I thought you'd lost your mind."

"But you wanted the sailboat."

"Sailing is beautiful, restful, and romantic. Of course, I wanted a sailboat, but I didn't suppose you'd ever take me seriously."

"Sailing is a skill; you'll learn it and so will all the kids."

"I can see now that you were wise. No matter where we go or what we do in the summer, they can't wait to get back to the lake."

"It will mean even more in years to come. It will be the one place we can afford to come. And there's always plenty of work to do," he said.

"The sun has been so good for Velvet. She doesn't have to worry about taking the weight off her leg in the water."

"Nothing like cold water swimming with no chemicals in the pool. I tighten up my flab in the summer long enough to last me through the winter . . . as long as I jog, of course."

"Randy, sometimes I think you're a little boy that won't ever grow up, but I have to admit, you keep us all sane. Laughter is our best medicine."

"Oh, that reminds me. I've got an idea for home evening next week."

"Randy . . ."

"Well, James has this playhouse up the canyon, an open-air theatre. He wants to promote family night fun. I told him we'd come up and do our Country Road song."

"You've got to be kidding."

"Why not. I'm getting pretty good on the guitar, and you can play the piano."

"Who'll do the singing?"

"We can all sing. We're the typical Mormon family who sings."

"I hope the kids will come through."

"They will; we'll just go for a ride and spring it on them."

"Oh, Randy, you are the craziest man."

"The reason you married me, right?"

"Right."

"Oh, and for the next week I've reserved some horses and a wagon. This old guy has a wagon box that he pulls with a matched team, and for a small fee he'll take us up the canyon to a church wagon lunch and bring us back. Sound fun?"

"Sounds crazy, but I'm sure the kids will like it."

"We've got to keep them laughing. I read a book last week that told how a man used laughter as medicine. He had this painful illness, and he found out if he laughed for fifteen minutes, he could sleep for two hours without pain. Do you believe that?"

"I do if you say so, Randy." Molaine chuckled as his eyes finally gave up trying to stay open, and she fell asleep on Randy's shoulder.

12

Velvet was on crutches all that time, and then suddenly the x-rays showed the bone had solidified, and she was through with the harness and crutches. The hurt and worry and heartache were over as quickly as it had appeared, and they were all left wiser and more understanding.

"She will probably always limp," the doctor said.

"Is there anything we can do to avoid that?"

"Therapy will help."

"What about modern dance?"

"Probably won't hurt."

"Then I think we'll give her modern dance lessons; they will be more fun and more profitable. Is there anything else we should do, Doctor?"

"We might consider operating."

"Why will you want to operate?"

"To shape the bone up. It might help with arthritis later in her life."

"Is that the only reason?"

"Yes."

"Then I think we won't operate now. We'll wait and take our chances with the later years. They may learn more."

"That's true. Bring her in for tests once in a while."

"I will, Doctor."

The day little Velvet stood in church without her crutches for the first time and talked to the many friends and neighbors that had been so thoughtful, she stole their hearts and filled their eyes with tears. "I want to thank everybody who prayed for me," she said, her face radiant. "I want to thank my family, to thank Heavenly Father for blessing me and making me better. I love Heavenly Father. He is so good to little children like me. Now I can learn to roller skate and ride my bike. Thanks, everybody; thanks, Heavenly Father."

That was all. She finished and walked back to her place beside her family, smiling happily. But the hush stayed in the chapel, broken only by quiet sobs of those who listened and cared.

And then the years seemed to fly. They were so full of activity and building that they seemed to go by like telephone poles on a desert road. There were wonderful carefree days when Randy came home early in the day, and they all went to a movie in the middle of the afternoon. There was the time Randy took his two oldest daughters shopping for cowboy boots and hats, with cap pistols for the Fourth of July, and little cowgirl skirts and fringed jackets Molaine made to go with the boots. There was Velvet in dance, Toni in Pep, PTAs, and work in the ward, in the garden, and in the yard. They were a busy family.

Molaine directed plays, worked in the Primary while the children were there, and then there were more jobs in MIA, so that she was ready for her children when they came into MIA. The things teenagers could think of to do were never any shock to Molaine; she had been through it all with others long before her own children hit the season.

There was teaching in the Relief Society, and Randy in the Bishopric, Randy as Bishop. Those were special years when Randy was Bishop.

The family didn't see Randy much when he became Bishop Randy, but when they did, Molaine realized he had so much more to give. Listening to people, he had become more atuned to problems and more grateful for his own family.

One day after church, Bishop Randy stepped into the hall to

greet his next appointment, and there sat little Randy.

"Bishop Randy," said little Randy, reaching up to shake the Bishop's hand, "I believe my appointment is next."

"Son, I'll be with you in a minute."

"Isn't my appointment next? The clerk told me to sit here."

"Oh, well, yes, I guess it is. Did you have something important to see me about?"

"Yes, Bishop. Can I come into your office and sit down like the other people do?"

"Of course, you can." The Bishop was surprised and amused. He walked into his office with his son following him, indicated a chair, and they both sat down. "Now, Brother Randy, Jr., what is it I can do for you?"

"I thought it would be nice to have an interview with my Bishop. You see Bishop, I have joined the little league football team, and I'll be starting as quarterback next Saturday. Do you think it's all right for me to accept the assignment?"

Bishop Randy smiled, the grin stealing around his lips, and his first reaction was to want to grab little Randy by the shoulders, give him a hug, and push him out the door to his practice. But since Little Randy was so serious, he offered his hand.

"Congratulations, Brother Randy. I think you will make a very fine quarterback. Can you get me season tickets to watch the games?"

"There won't be any charge, Bishop, but I think I'll be able to do a lot better job if you come and see me."

"I'll be glad to do that. Is that all you wanted to see me about?"

"Yeah, I guess so." Little Randy got up to leave, then turned and looked at his father. "Thanks for seeing me, Sir. Since I don't see you very often, I thought maybe it would be good to have an official interview the way the missionaries do. Is that all right, Sir?"

Bishop Randy held out his arms to his son, and little Randy went into them. His father hugged him tight.

"You know, son, I think this is a very good idea. Any time

you have anything to say to me just call the clerk, and he'll get you in. How did you manage to get the ball games scheduled on Saturday instead of Sunday?"

"It was a little trick of mine. I told them I couldn't play on Sunday and that my dad couldn't come and watch me on Sunday. Since a lot of the guys are Mormons, they went for the idea."

"Thanks, Dad."

"And Randy?"

"Yes, Sir."

"I think the idea of an appointment for an interview is a good idea. Let's do it again when you're ready."

"Yes, Sir."

After that, whenever little Randy was in the need of a father's council, he called the clerk and made an appointment.

And so little league games started, and the family was delighted. All but Jesica, who would much rather have stayed home to play with paper dolls. The family attended every football game, yelling and screaming to let Little Randy know they were there and that he had some fans counting on him while he played in rain and sun and snow, getting himself slick and drenched and bloody. He had a nose that took only a small bump to make it bloody, and it was bloody part of every game.

During little league season, just as it was starting up for fall games, as Little Randy was playing for the second year, Toni was suddenly a young lady and ready to leave home and go away to college. She was the oldest and the one Molaine had turned the family over to whenever she needed help. Molaine had to face the fact that Toni was on her way.

"I have loved your dating years, your teen years. You have always been obedient, and I haven't had any of the problems most mothers talk about, Toni. I'm going to miss you."

"I don't think I'm ready to go away, Mother."

"But you don't want to stay home, do you, Toni?"

"No. The boys are all going on missions, and all my girlfriends are going away to school. I want to go, but I don't." Toni looked close to tears.

"Don't worry, you'll love it. You'll love college. The boys

are more mature. The ones that are there are more serious about education. You'll have a riot and learn something besides."

"What will I do when we need to have one of our talks?"

"There's always the telephone and writing."

"Writing . . ." emphasized Randy, who worried about big phone bills.

"And I'm not so far away I can't come if you need me." Molaine put her arm around her daughter and hugged her.

"It's little Jesica I'll miss the most." Toni picked her up and cried as she hugged her.

"You've been like her mother, Toni. But she'll come and visit you when you have time for her."

"We should get on with life, shouldn't we, Father?" Toni looked at her father, repeating his words.

"That's right, Daughter, and . . . remember . . ."

"Remember who I am . . . I know, Father."

"You seem to have all the speeches down. You've chosen well in the past, Toni. You'll be prayerful and will choose well. Shall I give you a father's blessing?"

So the family was called together, and Toni received her blessing while her mother and grandmother cried, and afterwards Jesica refused to let go of Toni's neck.

"I can't believe the time is here." Molaine was close to tears in the middle of trying to be brave for her daughter. "We just got your room all finished the way you like it, and you're going away."

"I'll take over her room." Velvet was still following in her sister's footsteps.

"I'll want it when I come home."

"I wonder if you'll ever really be home to stay again? You'll be on your own except for the checkbook strings and the car."

"There will be summer vacation and Christmas, Mother."

"That's right. What am I worried about?"

And so Toni put all her things into the truck, and they drove her to college. Then Molaine came home to follow little league another season.

It was while Toni was away at the University and Randy

Norman was following the little league games that Molaine and Randy decided it was time to have their last baby.

"If I'm ever going to have another, it has to be now," Molaine said to Randy.

"Are you sure it's wise to have another child when you have a daughter in college?"

"Randy, it's a wonderful time. I'm more mature now and think how much fun Jesica has been. We need one more. I have felt for a long time that there is another member of our family all ready to come to us. We've been so busy that we've put off having one. Sometimes I've wondered if it's right to bring another one into this busy life. But I won't always be this busy."

"Are you sure, Molie?"

"Aren't you?"

"Yes, I think we should have another. Jesica needs someone to play with. There's too big a gap between Randy Norman and Jesica."

"And so they decided to have one more child. It was interesting the effect it had on the children. Molaine had been worried about how Toni would take the news when she was in college, but Toni was the most enthusiastic of all.

"A baby . . . I can't believe it. You and I could be having another one together, Mother."

"We could? Are you making an annoucement, Toni? Have you fallen in love?"

"No. I haven't found Mr. Wonderful yet, Mother. But I could. He could appear quite quickly, and then I could get married and within a year could have a baby."

"Well, let's get the wedding over first, huh? In fact, why not let me have a baby this year, and you fall in love next year?"

"Mother, I think you're old-fashioned," laughed Toni.

Velvet's reaction was a little different. "Oh, Mother, I'm afraid it might be embarrassing for some of my friends. They think more than one child is bad news."

"Oh, well, I'm sorry about your friends, Vel. What do you think I should do? Abortions are legal now."

"Mother, you wouldn't think of such a thing, would you?"

Molaine laughed. "Of course, I couldn't think of such a thing. You just sounded so funny. I'm crazy about having a baby. I haven't made up my mind if I want a boy or a girl, but I think I'll just take potluck and not worry about that. I just want a baby."

"I do, too. My friends will just have to understand."

"I'm glad you are going to handle your friends."

"They are funny sometimes, Mother, but I don't care. You have your baby, but I'm afraid I won't be much good as a sitter. I'm too busy with dance and other things."

"I have a feeling you'll make time for something as special as our baby. I remember how Toni made time for Jesica. I won't worry about you."

And so while Molaine got bigger and bigger, she went to more and more little league games for Randy Norman. He had long since given up the name of Little Randy, since he was getting bigger, and they couldn't keep older Randy and younger Randy separate, so they'd started using his second name and called him Randy Norman or just Norm.

Randy Norman's attitude about the baby thrilled Molaine the most. He seemed to enjoy calling attention to the baby even when his friends were around, and he loved spoiling his mother and pampering her . . . except of course, on game day. Everything moved back for game day.

And then the seasons of little league were over, and Randy Norman went on to play football in high school. His games had a way of holding the family together. Every Friday was a time to stop talking to Randy Norman in the morning. It was game day. He dressed in his best clothes and went to school, and it was strictly forbidden to talk to girls on game day. Friday was a nervous day, and Randy Norman wasn't himself until the gun went off, and the game started. Then he was all football player, driving down the field with determination that was to become symbolic of his life.

Somehow, the birth of baby Joel Norman was sandwiched in between games and seasons, and mother and baby went right on attending football games. Meanwhile, Randy Norman made a name for himself in football and later won a scholarship to college.

"On to the University to show them what you can do, huh, Son?" Randy put his arm around his son's shoulders while Molaine stood crying over his helmet that needed the crossbones and stars taken off so they could turn it in just after graduation.

"No, Dad. I hope you don't mind, but I won't be going out for football in college. I thought I wanted to go pro, but I'm not that big, and football, to me, is something you play in high school. When you go to college, you think of more important things. I'd like to go on a mission, Dad. Is that all right with you?"

Randy hugged his son again. "We've always hoped you'd go on a mission. Yes, son. We'll support you in those ideas."

The following year Randy Norman went on his mission, and Toni fell in love. There was a mission and a wedding the same summer.

"Randy, our lives are moving away from us. The children are all leaving."

"Isn't that what we raised them for?"

"I guess it is."

"We've been pretty blessed. We still have each other. Velvet has a limp, but she's a beautiful dancer. Jesica is big enough to be a baby sitter now, and little Joel is coming up ready for little league."

"It seems like we are always starting over."

"Life fills a pattern, doesn't it? We do something for our children that our parents did for us. We can never repay those who go before except by being a model for those who follow."

"We've loved our children only second to our God, Randy. That has been the key, hasn't it? To love Heavenly Father, to make Him the center of our lives. How often we could have been thrown off if we hadn't depended on faith in Christ and our Father."

"It takes a long time to understand that, doesn't it, Molaine?"

"Oh, how many times we have had to learn that. And now we are sending our son, the cream of the crop, away on from us to another country where we can't do anything for him except send him a check and depend on the Lord to protect him. This

Gospel has got to be true."

"Do I hear a doubt in your voice?"

"I don't know. I've always wanted a son to go on a mission, but now that the time is here, I wonder . . ."

"Another test of your faith, Molaine. Perhaps the biggest test of all."

"I wonder, Randy, I wonder . . ."

13

With Randy Norman in the Mission Training Center, on his way to France, Molaine could concentrate on Toni's wedding. Toni met Daniel Warburton at the University. To Molaine, it seemed like she had just written about him and then suddenly she was calling to make sure the family was home, and she brought him and the diamond on her finger at the same time. It wasn't quite that fast. He had been home to Sunday dinner a few times, but the family hadn't taken her dating seriously. After all, Toni had dated all through high school, and nothing ever came of those dates.

"I should have known he was a threat when I found out he was home from his mission. RM's are all set up for marriage. Their mission presidents do a good job of brainwashing them about all the advantages of marriage."

"It isn't like that, Mother," Toni protested. "We just met, without any plans of getting serious, and suddenly it was serious. You understand, don't you?"

Molaine looked at Randy, a light passed between them, and Molaine nodded. "I understand, dear. Now about the wedding?"

"We've got the wedding all planned. We've looked at colors and thought about the line. I hope you can afford it, Mother."

"Yes, I hope we can afford it, too, baby," Randy added as a silent listener who felt the need to get in a word.

"We do have a budget, you know."

"You won't scimp on my wedding, will you, Mother?"

"Not any more than we have to. We have a son on a mission, too. And even though he made some of his money before he left, we do have to keep him there."

"Well, let's not talk about money in front of Daniel. I have such a lovely ring. Don't you think so, Mother?"

"A lovely ring. Now what other plans have you made? Do we get to know about your plans?"

"I think I'm supposed to ask how you intend to support my daughter or something like that."

"Daddy, how could you?"

"I think somebody asked me that, didn't they, Molaine?"

"I can't remember. We were so broke. I think if anyone had asked me that, I might not have gotten married."

"Well, Sir," Daniel started to say, "I intend to work. I'll be out of school by the time we get married, and I should be able to find a good position."

"Of course, my boy. Anyway, that's your worry, once you take my daughter away."

"You aren't kicking me out already, are you, Daddy?"

"Of course not, baby." Randy put his arms around his daughter. "My goodness, I've forgotten how sensitive engaged couples are."

So the wedding plans were set, and preparation went into full swing. Remembering her own wedding and how confusing some decisions could be, Molaine tried to make Toni's wedding smoother, the transition easier. But in the end there were still hurt feelings that came from a difference of opinon.

"It's part of getting used to living with a person from another background and family," Molaine said to Randy while working on Toni's wedding dress. "I learned, and she can learn also. Daniel is a fine boy, but Toni will find out he has some ideas of his own that she will have to consider."

"Did I have ideas of my own?" Randy asked.

"Did you? When I think of some of the things I went through just to make you happy. . ."

"Why didn't you tell me?"

"I did, Randy. Sometimes you could see my point of view, and sometimes you couldn't."

"Was it that important? Why didn't you just tell me what you wanted. I wouldn't care."

Molaine laughed. "You probably wouldn't care that much now, but how would we know! We've become so much like each other I don't know what's your opinion and what's mine. I've learned when we differ, it's not that big of deal. It isn't you or me anymore, it's just us. I wonder when that took place?"

"Over the years. I wanted to be right for you so much. And then I found that it was more important just to be with you and have you happy that it wasn't so important to be right anymore, just happy."

"And yet if you had given in to me too much, I'd have thought you didn't care."

"What fools we mortals be. Wouldn't you hate to go back to that time that Toni and Daniel are going through? How would you like to start all over, Molie?"

"Not me. It's taken a long time to grow into my marriage. We both did a lot of changing."

"I guess we're still changing, but it's less painful now."

"We're kinda' set in our ways, but we're kinda' set together."

"Mother, I'm on my way to Primary," announced Jesica. "Toni and Daniel will drop me off."

"All right. I'll pick you up. If I'm a little late, walk over to your friend, Janet's. All right?"

"All right. I'll call you from there, just in case you forget."

"I won't forget."

But the day wore on. There were some phone calls. One from Daniel's parents on some problems that had to be solved about the wedding breakfast. Then Randy got a call from the ward; a member had taken ill, and he had to get to the hospital quickly. Molaine was having trouble with the veil of Toni's wedding dress, and then suddenly she looked at the clock and remembered Jesica.

"My word, I was supposed to pick her up. She hasn't called

me." She went to the phone to call Janet's mother. No one answered. "She isn't home. I should have called her when Jesica left to make sure she was home. But she's always been home on Primary day. Jesica always walks over to Janet's."

With wild thoughts of things she should have done running around in her mind, she wrapped Joel in a blanket and put him in his car seat, got in the car, and drove up to the church. It was dark. Everyone had gone, and the building was locked. Then Molaine drove to Janet's house, only a block away. It was also dark. She began to panic.

"Jesica, so little, where could she have gone? Why did I do it? Why didn't I call and make sure? Why didn't I pick her up on time?" The thoughts ran round and round in her head as she headed back toward home. "Maybe someone gave her a ride home." But when she got there, it was still quiet. Everyone had gone somewhere. Molaine began to panic. Back in the car, thinking the worst thoughts she'd ever had, seeing little Jesica on the street alone, seeing her ringing Janet's doorbell and no Janet.

"Janet has always been there. Why didn't I call?" Up and down the street, home and back again. Nothing. It was getting dark, and the night air was chilly. "Jesica only had a sweater," she said aloud. Then she drove in front of Janet's house, went into the neighbors next door, and called Randy's office to leave a message for him to come quickly.

"I guess I'd better call the police," she said to the neighbor.

"I haven't seen them all day. They left yesterday morning to go out of town, and I haven't seen them since."

Molaine felt desperation circle her emotions. "Where could one little girl be? I've been thinking about the wedding and every-thing else, but not about Jesica. I've got to call the police." In her heart she was praying desperately. "Please, Father, don't let anything happen to Jesica. I'm so sorry I'm neglectful; let her be all right, and I'll be a better mother. Truly, I will . . ." She made her way to the front gate of Janet's house with every intention of going next door to use the phone, but first, a thought slipped into her head. *The back door. I haven't checked the back door.*

Through the side gate and around to the back door of Janet's house, but nothing; all was quiet and dark. Molaine turned to leave. Something moved in the bushes, and a small voice said, "Mamma, is that you?"

"Jesica! Jesica!!" Molaine turned to see a small shivering little Jesica come out from behind a bush by the back door. She grabbed her in her arms and kissed her. "Jesica, I was so worried. I'm so sorry I was late picking you up."

"Janet wasn't home, Mother. I was afraid so I hid in the bush. I'm cold."

Together they went back to the car in the driveway of Janet's house where Joel waited sound asleep. It was over. Jesica was found. But the nightmares of what might have happened because of her bad timing and neglect were just starting for Molaine. She thought of all the things that had happened to children, children left alone. That night she spent a lot of time on her knees.

"Father, today could have been so different. What if I hadn't found her? Oh, Father, thank you for blessing me and undoing my mistakes." All the thoughts of memories and missions dropped into second and third place. For weeks to come, as she worked on the wedding dresses, Molaine's mind was full of what might have been.

"Only Father protects my children, and He has a full-time job," she related to Toni. "And only the Holy Ghost can let you know if you are marrying the right man or not. Do be prayerful, Toni. Marriage is a serious business; so many things can happen. So many things can't be planned. We are so small in this very large world, and only a loving Father can show us the way."

"I know, Mother. How do you suppose I found Daniel?"

14

The wedding was over, and Toni and Daniel were on their way. Randy and Molaine couldn't believe how many relatives and friends had come out for the event. The one sad thing was that Elder Randy Norman had missed the wedding of his oldest sister, and he was only a few miles away. But he was so caught up in the spirit of missionary work, he'd only talked about the wedding casually in a letter and then went on about all the spiritual experiences he was going through.

Not all of Randy Norman's friends had chosen to go on a mission. There was some hurt among their parents. One day, the parents of Scott, a boy that had played football all through high school with Randy Norman, called to talk to Randy and Molaine.

"How did you get your son to go on a mission?"

"I guess we always just expected him to go on a mission the same way we expected him to go to church with us." Bishop Randy smiled, but he knew the heartache of Scott's parents and how hard they had tried to get their son to go.

"I guess Randy and I were so busy trying to do the things we were supposed to do ourselves that the children just came along with us," Molaine explained. "And then we've always talked to the boys about their missions. It's a big event in our lives, one we all look forward to."

"My wife and I tried everything from bribery to force.

Nothing worked." Scott's father looked away, and the hurt in his eyes showed.

"I guess it's like our girls thinking about the temple. When they were little and played dress up in the front room, they would leave their dolls with me to tend (I was the grandmother, you know, even though I didn't like being called a grandmother in those days.) while they pretended they went to the temple. They didn't even know what the temple was. They only knew that Randy and I got baby sitters while we went to the temple."

"Maybe that's the difference." Scott's mother shook her head. "We didn't go to the temple very often. I was always working. We did go to church. But it seems like you didn't ever have to worry about your children, Bishop." Randy and Molaine looked at each other.

"Oh, we worried," said the Bishop.

"And we prayed," added Molaine. "There were times I didn't get up off my knees, and I was never sure just what plans the Lord had that were different than mine. I worried most of the time that I wouldn't do what was right for them. And the story isn't over yet. I always wonder if they'll find their own faith, get their own testimony of the guidance of the Spirit. It takes a lifetime of testing to find the answers, and just when I think I've got it all figured out, there's another bridge to cross, one I hadn't planned on and don't understand. But I do have a testimony of our Father in Heaven and that he cares about us all."

"We tried to keep our family together, but the closer we pulled them, the harder they'd fight to get away. I don't know what we did wrong. What is your magic formula?"

"Magic formula? I wish I had one." Randy thought a minute. "Let me say that the only magic I know is clinging to Father in Heaven for direction. Nothing else works. And not all prayers are answered in a positive way but for our best good. If we look at each situation, there are great blessings to be gained. My wife is better at the positive handle to every situation than I am. She makes it work."

They talked a little more and then parted, and Randy and Molaine pondered the hurt of their friends and wanted to help but didn't know how.

"Scott's parents seem so worn out. Mental exhaustion is more difficult than physical."

"Scott's a good boy. Do you think he'll ever shape up and go on a mission?"

"He'd like to. Ironically, he's afraid of hurting his parents even more. He thinks if he talks about a mission and builds their hopes, then decides not to go, it would hurt them worse."

"That's a cop out excuse."

"I know, but he justifies himself that way. Molie, children love their parents and want to please them. It's just that when they feel threatened, they fight against those they love the most."

"Somebody should talk to him."

"Do you want to do it?"

"No, it isn't my place to try to change his mind."

"I guess it's all our places. Every member a missionary. But if we push too hard, we turn them away faster than we bring them in. A thin line. Molie, what do you think our strongest help with our children has been? Just between you and me."

"Talking things out together. My hardest time in all my life has been when we didn't see each other every day and talk. And we've always admitted to each other that we were dependent upon our Father in Heaven. To make decisions together based on His life as our model. I think those are the times when we've been strong and effective."

"That hasn't always been easy to do."

"Hasn't always been . . . you mean isn't *now* easy to do. We aren't through yet, Randy. We'll never be through raising children."

"One married and on her way."

"You think marriage is the end of our responsibility?"

"Most of it."

"Now we need to be models more than ever before. We can't teach our children what we've learned and expect them to accept it. We have to show them it works."

"Come on, Molie. We're almost home free. Don't get too involved in our children's lives. They are capable of their own decisions once they leave home."

"Funny man. You'll see. Only it's harder when we haven't jurisdiction."

And so it wasn't over. New experiences brought new worries and responsibility, and they found having a missionary son wasn't the same as going on a mission yourself or waiting for a missionary. And Molaine found out that married daughters need to talk even more than unmarried daughters, and her job was to be there to listen. Not to talk, mostly just to listen. And they became a family that ran for the mail. A letter from Toni and Daniel, a letter from Elder Randy Norman, and as they read the letters together, the unity of the family remained strong. Letters were like a drug of delight that made them all feel the communication they were afraid was slipping away.

While Randy Norman was on his mission, his father, Bishop Randy, was released from the Bishopric and given a job teaching a Sunday School class. It was like a demotion at first, a demotion that worried Randy. He'd been so involved in lives he wondered if he could go back to just being a teacher.

"It's another test, Molaine," Randy said one day after Sunday School, after giving what he considered a worthy lesson. "This is the big one for a lot of men. The change from the Bishop to being thrown back into the pond with all the other fish. I was lost at first. But you know what? I like it, Molie. I like teaching those kids eye-to-eye again. Makes me feel young. A teacher. And me at the crucial forties, when a lot of men go astray and try to recapture their youth. This is a good way to recapture my youth, being one of the kids. I wish Joel would hurry and get into football while I'm still able to make it to the games. Be good to me, Molaine. I'm in the terrible forties, the dangerous years."

Molaine laughed. "They are just as dangerous for me. I'm getting older, too. Aren't you worried about me?"

"When we have to worry about you, we are all lost. If you don't make the kingdom, none of us will. I'm counting on you to put in a good word for me."

"Look who's talking. You're the patriarch of our family. You'll pull me through."

"No. Men hold the Priesthood, but women have that special power of wife and mother. I've counseled enough people to know that women are usually the ones who make marriages work. Following the Priesthood is no easy task, and it's the basis of marriage."

"But only when the man doesn't use his authority unjustly. He has to be a man guided by the Spirit."

"Mom," said Velvet who had been listening through her studies, "did you and Dad ever think about a divorce?"

"Oh, I guess there were times I was upset enough that I might have left your father, at least for a few days, but I didn't have any money, and by the time I got some money I didn't want to go."

"You bet," added Randy. "Marriage is never easy. That's why you have to be so careful who you decide on."

"I think I'll wait and see who decides on me."

"Just make sure you attract the right kind, Velvet, and then test him out with the rules."

"The rules aren't that easy to test. I see a lot of Toni's friends making big mistakes."

"Only staying close to the guidance of the Spirit can warn you. When I think of how much I didn't know about your father when I married him, it's frightening."

"Mom, if marriage is so hard, how is it that you and Dad stayed together?" Randy and Molaine looked at each other again.

"Well, little daughter," said Randy, "we were too busy to worry about divorce. We had lots of problems to solve, a house to buy, a car to get, and all you kids to feed and get into school. We didn't have time to think about divorce."

Molaine laughed, and then they all joined in.

"Well, just as long as you don't get a divorce after you get us all raised. That's what some people do. Can you believe a grandma and grandpa getting divorced? Eileen's grandparents are getting a divorce."

"After coming that far together?"

"She says they never did get along, and now they've decided to go their own way."

"Oh, my goodness. Randy, you don't suppose that could ever happen to us, do you? I mean when we get all our work done?"

"We'll never get our work done. We're going to travel and see the world when we get the children raised. Besides, I'll still be working. I've got to have money."

"That's true. I'm looking forward to being able to do all the things I haven't had time to do while the kids are keeping us busy. I want to study and paint and do some genealogy."

"How dull, Mother. I know we are supposed to do our genealogy, but I've never really wanted to."

"Oh, it's fascinating. I find the most interesting stories about our ancestors. It sounds dull, but it isn't dull at all. I want to go to England and see where my people started out."

"I could go for going to England, Mother."

"No, Vel." Randy reached over to touch Vel's long hair effectionately. "You haven't earned your trip yet. You have to work and raise your family first, then you can travel. Your mother and I have earned our rest. At least we probably will have earned it by the time we get all of you raised."

"And just think, your father and I will have time to talk and be together without having to schedule a time for ourselves. We'll just do everything together. It should be a wonderful time, don't you think, Randy? What's that song about when the kids get married?"

"We don't have to worry about that yet. We still have Vel's dance concert to go to, Jesica's play at school, feed Joel eight times a day, and you know the latest?"

"What's the latest?" Vel sat up straight, ready to listen. Her father didn't often make an announcement, but when he did, it was usually one worth listening to.

"Last night your mother and I got a call from Toni. It seems we are soon to be grandparents. Toni is going to be a mother."

"And Daniel a father!!"

"That's usually the procedure."

"Hurrah. I'll be an aunt."

"Will I be an aunt, too?" asked Jesica, coming into the room to kiss her parents goodnight again."

"You'll be a small, sweet little aunt." Molaine held out her arms and snuggled her small daughter close.

It was a special time. The family hurried to the mailbox everyday for a letter from Elder Randy Norman or Mrs. Daniel who was having a baby. It was a special time, and yet there was more time for those who were left at home. Velvet had used her therapy dancing to good advantage and found she had a real talent and decided to not only take dance lessons but teach them as well. She had a group of little children in the neighborhood, and with her father's help she was able to turn the basement of the new McGregary home into a dance studio. Her prize student was, of course, Jesica, who was always bubbly and excited about everything she did.

"Randy, our Velvet has been blessed in ways we couldn't foresee." Molaine watched the dance concert proudly. "We might never have given her dancing lessons if it hadn't been for her hip."

"Blessings come in ways we least expect them." Randy reached for his wife's hand, an action that always made Molaine feel young and still loved. "Just ask me. I'm a man that has learned how great it is to be a Sunday School teacher. Every man needs to rise to Bishop and then find fruits of labor in less glamorous church work. There are a lot of people who come up through the ranks of the Church and never get a testimony of the Gospel. Do you know that, Molie?"

"I've found that out. A lot of people work in the Church and never really learn about the Gospel. The true Gospel comes from within, not from which church calling you have. Our Elder Randy Norman has found that truth already."

The days of life seemed to fly faster as Randy and Molaine got older. Before Randy Norman came home from his mission, Toni had a baby boy. He was born six weeks before he was expected, and a fast call in the middle of the night got Randy and Molaine on a plane, carrying them to the side of their married daughter.

"Just when everything was going so well. I'm worried about Toni. She hasn't really had very much to endure in her life,

Randy."

"How much had you had when we were first married?"

"But I'd hate to go through all that again."

"But you had your chance to learn. Would you take away that chance from Toni?"

"What are you saying, Randy? Are you worried about the baby?"

"I could tell Daniel was worried when he called."

"What will Toni do if anything happens to her baby? Oh, Randy, pray for them. Pray really hard for them."

15

"**R**andy, it's harder to watch the children go through the heartaches than it is to go through them myself."

"I hadn't planned on this. Toni was so happy with marriage and the idea of being a mother. She was married right. She didn't ever think of being married anyplace but the temple. She married the right kind of man. Having a baby is a righteous desire. Surely our Father will bless this baby."

"Randy, you're more worried than I thought. You haven't given up hope, have you?"

"The baby's breathing isn't good, and when the doctor talked to me, he tried to prepare me. I could tell that. He expects me to prepare the parents."

"If we only knew which way to prepare them. There isn't anything we can do but just be here."

"I guess that's the best for now. The kids are so young, they don't sense the danger until it hits them in the face."

"That's a blessing, Randy. I was glad to go through my growing experiences one at a time."

"I wish I could feel stronger about the little boy the way I felt about Randy Norman when he was born. But to watch him struggling for breath. I have a bad feeling."

Randy reached for Molaine's hand, and they walked down the hall together, back and forth. Walking seemed to help the waiting. Daniel was with Toni. Then as they settled back down in the waiting room, the doctor came to find them.

"The baby isn't doing very well. I think if you want the boy to have a name, it would be a good idea to name him within the next hour. Would you like to tell the parents, or would you like me to do it?"

Randy shook his head. "No, Doctor. I'll tell them. You think it should be within the hour?"

"That's my best advice."

Molaine began to shake as if a cold wind had suddenly started blowing. She reached for Randy's hand, but he was gone. He had gone to get Daniel.

"Have you chosen a name for your son, Daniel?" Randy put his arm around Daniel's shoulders after he'd called him into the hall out of Toni's room.

"We've thought of girls' names mostly. Toni was so sure she was having a girl."

"Can you talk to her and decide on a name right away? I can call your Bishop for you."

Daniel looked at Randy quickly. "Then you think he won't make it?"

"The doctor suggests we name him now just in case. He's struggling for air."

"Isn't there anything they can do? It will kill Toni if she can't have her baby."

"She's a strong girl, Daniel. We won't give up. But the doctor did suggest . . ."

"I'll talk to Toni. I don't know how I'm going to tell her."

"Do you want me to tell her?"

"No, Sir, that's my job. I'll tell her. But don't go away. I'm sure she'll want to talk to you."

"We aren't going anywhere, son. We'll be right here."

Daniel went back into the room, and Randy put his arm around Molaine's shivering shoulders. "This is going to be a hard one. Come and help me look up the telephone number of Daniel's Bishop. I haven't got my glasses, and I can't see through tears."

Within the hour Toni and Daniel had decided on a name, the Bishop arrived, and the baby was blessed and named. They named their little boy Daniel Randolph. And Toni, in a wheelchair, sat beside the bed of her little son and watched and prayed as they gave him his name. He'd already been given a blessing pertaining to his health. Randy had helped Daniel do that when he first arrived. Now they all stood beside him and watched his labored breathing. Toni put her finger inside his little hand, and he held on.

"Darling, you are trying so hard to hang on. I'm proud of you for that. You are such a good little boy. I would so like to have you stay with me and your father, and I know you are trying so hard. But you are tired, aren't you, little Daniel?" There were no tears in Toni's voice, just gentleness, the way a mother talks to her baby. "You've been with me for almost eight months. I'm sorry you were so anxious to get to us. You just needed to hurry up your mission here, didn't you?" She looked up at her husband, they both looked so mature in comparison to the two young people who had been so young and carefree less than a year before when they were married. "Honey." Toni went on looking first at her husband and then her small son. "I think little Daniel wants to go back to Heavenly Father. It's just too hard for him to stay with us. Shall we let him go?"

"Whatever he has to do to complete his mission here. We want what's best for him, don't we?" Toni leaned her head against her young husband, and her eyes were on her small son, her finger still in his hand. Do you want to go back to Heavenly Father, little son?" The baby opened his eyes and looked at his parents as if he understood, as if for him, time stood still a moment. He seemed to breathe easier. Toni's voice went on. "If you can't stay, if you have more important things to do for us all on the other side, then you can go back."

That was all she said, then they watched as the tiny eyes closed, and the little fingers relaxed their hold on his mother's finger. His breathing was gone; only the machinery went on. Toni sat there for a long time until the doctor came to shut off the machinery. Then she slumped forward in the wheelchair, and a nurse took her back to her room.

"Molaine, strangely I feel comforted, as if this was right for little Daniel. I feel like our prayers have been answered, and he is where he was called to be."

"I know, Randy, but my heart aches so much. I'm thinking of all those days ahead for Toni when she looks at the baby clothes and the little room she's fixed. I'm thinking of all the sweetness and heartaches they would have had together." Molaine broke down, her tears rushing forward in a flood.

"There will be some hard days ahead, but we have a daughter that has suddenly become a woman, with the heart of a woman and the good sense of a daughter of God. She'll hurt, Molie, but she'll be all right. And she has a husband who carries his responsibilities, a man who holds the Priesthood that she can lean on. I wondered how strong they were in their faith, remember? Well, now I know. We've raised some good children, Molie. There aren't any hurts too big to stand when you know you've raised children who will be obedient to our Father in Heaven."

Molaine nodded, wiping the tears from her eyes as she covered her mouth with her handkerchief. "I've got to get my crying over now, Randy. Toni will need some moral support when she begins to awaken. She's numb now and helped by the goodness of a small boy she carried inside herself for many months. But there will be times ahead when she needs to borrow our faith. We've got to be ready for that."

"We'll be ready, Molie."

"We never get through raising children do we, Randy?"

"I guess not. I attended a class on child raising last Sunday, and I thought I was wasting my time because our children were almost raised. I guess we go on learning so that someday we might have enough knowledge to be mothers and fathers of spirit children to be born into other worlds. It's something to live for, isn't it, Molie?"

"It's something to live for, Randy." She put her hand over her heart. "It hurts so bad, Randy. I remember the night of our accident, when we were on our honeymoon, and I thought you might be leaving me. I had a pain like this, then. I grew up that night. I turned my life over to my Heavenly Father, and I've never been sorry. I watched Toni turn her life and her son's life over to Heavenly Father, tonight."

"The hurt will last a long time. I guess it will never go away, but she's young; there will be more children. She's a happy person, there will be laughter and good times again. There will be summers at the lake together. The hurt will eventually turn into a dull pain. She will laugh again."

"I know, Randy. I know. Laughter and tears, the best years . . . we learn when we hurt, we grow when we conquer. We have more to give when we learn to endure. We can survive with laughter behind the tears. These really are the best years, Randy. But, oh . . . they are so confusing, and they hurt so much."